PRISONER
OF
THE
HEART

By

Annette DeLore

Publish America
Baltimore

First printing

ISBN: 1-59129-304-9
PUBLISHED BY PUBLISH AMERICA BOOK PUBLISHERS
www.publishamerica.com
Baltimore

Printed in the United States of America

This book is dedicated to my husband,
Dave
and our children,
Jamie, Karie, Timothy and Tarie.
Special thanks to my youngest daughter,
Tarie,
for her many hours of reading what I had written
and for being my sounding board.
Hope your ears ok!
I would also like to thank her for being my computer whiz,
you know what Mom means.

I would also like to thank my Mother,
Georgia Morningstar,
for without her first computer that she left at my house,
Prisoner Of The Heart would have never been put down on
paper,
(with my handwriting no one could have ever read it!)
I would also like to thank her for her support
when my first computer got hit by lighting, she got me up
and running again. Thanks Mom!

Chapter 1

As she ran out of the cabin, dragging the boy by the arm and heading for the car, Dakota knew he only had seconds to save the boy. It didn't matter to Dakota at this point his cover would be blown wide open. Not to mention the United States government would be down on his case. Saving Scott was all that mattered now.

With these thoughts on his mind, Dakota moved quickly from the edge of the Forrest and over to the car. He surprised the woman as he grabbed her by the arm, "Let the boy go, Liz!" In her surprise of being grabbed she released Scott.

"Run, Scott, Run," Dakota yelled.

"Dad," Scott screamed, knowing his father's voice.

"What are you doing here?" Liz looked at Dakota with shock.

"It's over Liz, you and Tom will be spending the rest of your life in prison," Dakota said.

The truth of Dakota's words sunk in. "I'm not going to prison for him or anyone," Liz shouted. The next few moments were slow motion to Dakota. Liz pulled out a small pistol and shot Dakota at point blank range, right in his chest.

The impact was unbelievable, the power of the pistol caused Dakota to take a few steps back. As he grabbed his chest, things started to spin around him. Somehow he knew that he fell and hit the ground. As the darkness started to close in on Dakota, his life flashed before his eyes. . . .

1978

As the fog became clearer, Dakota could see he was back on the aircraft carrier. A man was approaching him with the captain of the ship. "Airman Deer, this is Mr.Stanfield. If you have a few minutes, he would like to talk to you," Captain

Moore said.

"Sir? Yes Sir," Dakota answered his Captain. Looking at Mr. Stanfield he said, "Sir, how can I help you?"

"Call me Harold, Airman Deer." Then looking at the Captain, Harold continued, "Captain Moore, is there someplace private where the Airman and I could talk?"

"Yes Sir, I'll show you and Airman Deer to my Quarters, you can talk privately there," Captain Moore answered him.

Once in the captain's quarters Dakota was baffled. Seeing Dakota's wondering expression Harold said, "Sit down, Airman." As Dakota sat down Harold continued, "My name is Harold Stanfield. I work for the United States government, in the Secret Service, or a branch of it, I should say. We've been watching you for quite some time Airman Deer." Dakota didn't move a muscle. Harold continued. "And you have the qualifications we're looking for in an agent." Harold stopped there letting this information sink in for Dakota. The blank expression on Dakota's face was unreadable to Harold. *"Silent and thinking, he's going to make a fine agent,"* Harold thought. When Dakota spoke up after a few moments he said, "Sir, I'm interested, so what more can you tell me?"

"First of all if you join the Secret Service, we will want you sign a twenty-year contract. You will be paid well for you service to your country. As far as the Air Force is concerned you will be getting an early out, and an honorable discharge. We'd like you to go through training and then under cover."

"And when do you plan to do all of this?" Dakota asked.

"That depends on you, Airman Deer. First of all, your training will be with me. Since we will be partners, I suggest we use first names."

"Yes Sir, I mean Harold. My first name is Dakota. I'm ready for this whenever you can arrange it."

"I want to explain one more thing to you Dakota. Your undercover assignment will be in prison. You will be posing as an inmate, for first-degree murder, with a life sentence, however you won't be at the prison all the time. I'll explain the details to you later during training, but no one must know you are anything but an inmate. Not your family or friends, everyone you know and care about, will for the next twenty years only know you as inmate Deer. Can you handle this?"

Taking a few minutes to think about what Harold and the government were offering him, Dakota answered, "Yes, I think I can do this. But I sure do hope the pay is good." Harold laughed, "Dakota, the pay is great!"

A few weeks after the meeting with Harold, Dakota received an honorable discharge from the Air Force. He was then flown to Washington, D.C. to the C.I.A. building. In a brief meeting with Harold, the arrangements for the training and undercover life were explained. "We know this will be a rough life Dakota, so we want you to take six months, go back home, enjoy yourself and then I'll give you a call and our work will begin."

"Yes Sir, Harold," Dakota said smiling.

On Dakota's flight back to Michigan, he thought about all the things that had happened in the past few weeks and how his life was about to change.

He knew his mom would be waiting at the airport in Grand Rapids to pick him up. It had been two years since he had last seen his family. As far as they were concerned he was flying home from England, where he had been stationed with the Air Force.

The six months at home flew by fast. Dakota had touched base with his old friends from high school, had gotten a job, dated a few women and was having the time of his life. One evening while having a quiet dinner at home with his parents, the phone rang.

"I'll get it," Dakota told both his parents.

"Which lady is calling you now?" Dakota's mom teased as he reached for the phone.

"Could be one of many," Dakota answered with a hint of laughter to his voice. "Good evening," Dakota said as he picked up the phone.

"Hello, may I talk to Dakota please?" the voice on the other end said.

"Dakota speaking."

"Dakota, this is Harold. How have you been?"

"Just fine Harold and how about you? Hang on a minute." Then turning to his parents he said, "It's Harold, an old Air Force buddy of mine." Walking towards the living room Dakota continued. "So Harold, what have you been up to these past few months, since you got out?"

"Can you talk?" Harold said.

"I can now, I'm in the living room. Go ahead," Dakota said.

"A week from today, meet me at the Grand Rapids airport. I'll be at the luggage pick-up. Let's say at four p.m. From there we go to the training point." Dakota turned and saw his mother walk into the living room. "That sounds like a really good job. I can make more there in six months, than I can here in two years. I'll head out there next week. Thanks bud. See you soon."

Hanging up the phone, Dakota turned to his mother. "Harold called to offer me a job. I'll be working on oilrigs in Texas. The pay is four times as much as I can make here. They give us a place to stay, rent-free. I'm heading down there next week. I'll be gone for about six months to a year. Maybe I can even save enough money to build that house I want," Dakota said sounding excited.

"Oh! I hate to see you go. Dakota, I understand that you're grown up, but remember that you'll always be my boy. You will come home for Christmas won't you?" Cheryl said, sounding sad that Dakota was leaving. Dakota walked over, took his mother in his arms and gave her a kiss on the check. "Mom, I'll be home for Christmas, I love you mom."

Chapter 2

Seven months later . . .

Dakota called his mom in Michigan. "Mom, I've been arrested."

"What? Dakota where are you? What happened?" Cheryl sounded shocked.

"I've been arrested for First Degree Murder," he said. No sound came over the phone; all he could hear was air.

"God, Mom you there?" Then he heard the crying, "Mom are you all right?" Dakota asked. She was crying so hard, she could barely speak.

"Murder! My God Dakota, how could this be happening?" she cried, trying to catch her breath.

His stomach was in knots. He felt like throwing up. Even though there was a cool breeze he was sweating! *"How can I be doing this to my mom,"* he thought? There's no other way, they all have to believe I'm in prison.

"It's a long story. Mom, I've already been arraigned, but I don't know when the trial will be. I'll let you know when it's over."

As he spoke she regained her composure. Now anger set in. He acted like he had called to tell her he had just gotten a speeding ticket. "What the hell do you mean, you'll call me when it's over? We need to get you a good lawyer. I'll fly right down there," she exclaimed.

"No Mom, I got myself into this, and I can handle it. Trust me. I know what I'm doing. I've got a lawyer, and everything is going to be all right." He knew this would put her into a tailspin, but she couldn't come down, not now, not for a long time. She had to believe; they all did. "Mom, I'll call you in a few days. They say I have to get off the phone now, my time's up. I'll be ok. I love you Mom," with that he hung up.

Dakota knew he was putting his mother threw hell, but somehow he would make this as easy as possible on her.

The so-called "trial" came and went. She never made it to that, and he got sentenced to life in prison.

Dakota was placed at the Dog Pen on the penitentiary grounds, which was about two miles from the main prison. Dakota's job was working with the different breeds of dogs, training them to be K-9 cops. Each dog had a special use and Dakota's favorite to work with was the bomb and attack dogs. Along with six other inmates, Dakota worked ten-hour days. At night when the work was done, the inmates would return to the house the prison provided for them. To live at the Dog Pen, an inmate would have to be a trustee, with a sentence of fifteen years to life.

There were benefits living at the Dog Pen. A wood shop was provided for the inmates so they could work on hobbies. A few inmates would build furniture, while others were creative in wood-burning pictures. A fitness room with a weight bench and weights, along with a few workout machines was in the basement of the home. The phone in the house provided the inmates with contact to the outside world. It was as close to a normal life any inmate would ever see.

"Hey, so what's new up north?" Dakota asked his mom.

"Oh lots of snow and you should see all the deer and the wild turkeys we have behind the house. Dakota, you just wouldn't believe it. They just come right up to the door."

"Send me pictures Mom, I'd like to see that," Dakota said smiling to himself. If she had only known, he had seen the deer, turkeys, and his family quite often, only from a distance. Being an agent had its advantages.

"So what have you been up to? How's the woodworking going?" Cheryl asked him.

"I've been really busy. I've got so many orders for my wood plates, I don't know if I'll get them all done by Christmas," Dakota said.

"Rich and I plan on coming down at Christmas. Is there anything we can bring you?"

"Thanks Mom, but I've got everything I need. You might want to bring pictures of everyone up there, that would be great."

"Well I can't stay on the phone long, Mom. The boss has a few things he wants me to do today. I'll call you in a couple of weeks. Tell everyone I love them."

The "boss" was waiting for Dakota at the dog pen. "So what do you think of the new litter?" Bubba asked.

"Well I think we'll have a few good drug dogs and maybe even a tracker or two," answered Dakota. This litter was special. They were bred from the finest Curs.

After a period of time it was Dakota's job to train only the finest drug, tracking, bomb, and attack dogs. If he wasn't busy doing this, he was training agents from all over the country with their own K-9's. Dakota was one of the top trainers in the world and highly in demand. *"All this from prison,"* he would laugh at himself.

In Dakota's spare time, over the years, he had picked up a few hobbies. He started to draw and wood-burn pictures. After that, he went on to building furniture.

Some of the finest pieces of furniture were sold to senators with even the governor owning a few pieces. The word got around that if you wanted a good piece of "wood" you'd have to get it from "The Chief."

Knowing the prison arts and craft show, which was called the rodeo, was only a few days away, Dakota thought he'd go check on Chew. When he walked into the wood shop he spotted Chew working on a fancy wooden coat rack.

Chew was the only inmate Dakota was friends with. A large, muscular black man, Chew stood about six foot and weighed 240 lbs. Chew was in for life and was a trustee, but still he was not a man to mess with.

"Hey, Chew, what ya got ready for the rodeo?"

"Well, Mr. Dakota Chief," Chew said with a wide grin, "I thought Chitlings would be a good start. I's knows how ya'll mixed breed folk are. Can't make up your mind, if you be a Savage Injun, or a white boy. So me's figure Chitlings would put a little of that black soul into ya. Then we's just call ya a Heinz 57, be any breed ya want then." Dakota almost busted a gut laughing at Chew.

"Fuck You, Chew!" Chew made a playful straight face, "Dakota, ya'll not my type, ya'll have to go down to Main Camp, C block for that."

Dakota was the serious type, and Chew was the only person in a prison of over 2,000 inmates that could make Dakota laugh. Chew was 15 years older than Dakota and would tell him, "In a place like this, ya ain't got nothing else boy. If ya don't laugh once in a while, ya might as well be dead."

Chapter 3

"I left my first husband and I can leave you too!" she screamed. He was up in a flash, grabbing her by the throat, picking her up off her feet and banging her head into the wall, nearly knocking her out.

This man was like Dr. Jekyll and Mr. Hyde. She never knew what would come next. But this time, she told herself, was the last time. She was not going to live any longer with a mad man. The next time he just might kill her! Where would that leave the children?

It was time for work. As he was getting ready to leave, she wouldn't even look at him. Then the same old words came. "I'm sorry. Are you all right? I just don't know what came over me. It'll never happen again. I promise." But this time he added something different at the end. He took his hand, tilted her head up and looked her dead in the eye "You know I love you. I could never live without you. If you ever leave me, I'll find you and kill you!" With that he walked out the door.

Dawn knew he was telling her the truth, "He'd do it!" she told herself, "but if I stay here, he'll do it anyway, I've got to get away."

For the next few weeks Dawn walked on eggshells around Tom. Things seemed normal to Tom. He had acted as though he had forgotten all about his harsh words.

Dawn's life with Tom for the past five years had been a living hell. She never knew what might set him off. She did her best to live up to his idea of a good wife. The house was spotless. Daily dinner was promptly on the table at one in the afternoon. She never back talked to Tom.

She waited on him, hand and foot, but if she didn't move fast enough or if some small thing wasn't to his liking, he'd fly off the handle.

These outbursts over the years had left her with cracked ribs, a dislocated shoulder and a scar above her left eye, from the time he had hit her with his brief case. Worst were the rapes, and the many times he had hurt her with oral sex.

Dawn turned over and over in her mind possible ways out. This was not something that could be done overnight. Where could she go? Then it came to her, the perfect plan.

Carefully choosing a day when Tome was in a good mood, Dawn said. "You know Tom, the kids will be getting out of school for the summer in a couple weeks. Your mom called and wanted to know if the kids could come up again this summer for a week."

"Sure, you can take two of them up, drop them off. You and the other kids can be back by ten, no later than eleven that night." He knew this wouldn't give her much time, as it was a four-hour drive one way. "Then if Grandma is feeling up to it the following weekend you can go up and get the two oldest ones, and drop off the youngest two for a week."

Tom knew well the game of "Control" and how to play with one's mind. Never did he allow her to go and visit anyone alone. He would see to it that none of their family back home would know what was really going on. As far as they were concerned, Tom and Dawn were a very happily married couple. They'd been married for almost ten years and had four wonderful children. They were upstanding members of the Hope Baptist Church. Dawn was a member of the ladies' bible study, meeting once a week. Tom was a "great father, husband, and provider" as far as anyone on the outside knew.

Hoping her prayers had been answered she said, "Muggs" (her older sister's nickname) was wondering if maybe, while Grandma had two of the kids for a week, that maybe she could have the other two for the same week. Muggs said she'd take her two out to Grandma's when the week was done and she would trade kids with Grandma for the next week." Before he had time to say "No" to this, she went on, "If the kids were all gone for two weeks, I could get a lot of work done. You know I could paint the walls in the living room, shampoo the carpets, wash the outside of the house, and clean the basement. I could bring you supper at work. You know how you enjoy that." When he didn't reply Dawn's heart was sinking. As she silently prayed, "If you're listening God, please help me. I need to get away, before this madman kills me." Was God listening to her silent prayer?

Tom was also thinking to himself, "This would be a good time to teach her a lesson, or, she just might have an accident." A devilish smile slowly crossed his face, *"After all people die every day from accidents."* Then out loud he said to Dawn, "I think it's a good idea. Two weeks alone with you, my dear, is all I need."

Seeing the look on his face and the tone in his voice, Dawn knew she had better pray a silent prayer, "Dear God, please just give me a sign. If I am to leave this man, and it is your will, please help me and show me somehow, someway. I know that I am asking a lot Father, by asking you to give me a sign, but Lord, I really need to see something so I'll be sure it's ok with you. If it's not ok Lord, then I'll paint the room, clean the carpet, and try to be a better wife. In Jesus name I ask, Amen."

During the next few weeks Dawn kept very busy. The house was being packed up and readied for the painting and the carpet cleaning. Tom had decided that two weeks was more than enough time for Dawn to paint every room, not just the living room. The house that the Browns lived in was a very large ranch-style house. Complete with three bedrooms, two bathrooms, a kitchen, dinning room, a large sunroom, a full finished basement, and a breezeway, (the large room connecting the house to the garage.) The two-car garage was finished right down to having curtains and pictures.

The first room Dawn started in was the basement. This was no ordinary basement. It was like walking into a very elite nightclub. The L-shaped bar was on the left, made out of the prettiest walnut. A raised foot ledge and padded rail completed the rich look. It would comfortably seat 15 men. Behind the bar was a mirror, with a buck and doe standing outside the woods on a riverbank etched into the glass. When the dim lightning was on the picture appeared to come to life. The walls of the room were walnut halfway up, then textured the rest. At the far end of the room was a massive deep red brick fireplace with a mantel made of marble. The hearth was made of cut rock and was about 6 feet long and 3 feet wide. On either side of the fireplace were three diagonally long rectangular mirrors. The walls were decorated with walnut shelves upon which sat wildlife sculptures. With antique oil lamps glowing, the recessed lighting and a fire in the fireplace, one would expect to have a feeling of warmth and comfort.

But Dawn hated this room. It held nothing but bad memories for her. The memory of the many parties Tom had down there made her sick. She was forced to play waitress for his friends. After a few drinks the grabbing and fondling would start. If she resisted his friends and offended them, Tom would beat her later for embarrassing him. If she put up with their touching, Tom would accuse her of liking it. Then the sexual torture would start, to prove he was a better man.

Pushing the bad thoughts out of her mind, Dawn continued her work. In a couple of hours she had the basement packed up and ready to be painted. Several boxes were now ready to be taken up stairs and put into the sunroom for storage during the painting. At the last moment, Dawn decided these boxes should be marked, "Tom."

The next room was the girls' bedroom. In here she sorted through the clothes that were too small for the girls to wear. These she packed and marked for the church. Winter clothes went into boxes marked, "Winter Girls." Toys went into boxes also. Next the girls' clothes were packed for their stay with Grandma and Aunt Mugg's.

Her son's room was much easier, as there was only one of

him. The task only took Dawn about one hour in his room. His boxes were marked in the same manner as the girls'.

Dawn was now in her and Tom's room. She smiled when doing the closet. Taking her clothes out of it felt like a little bit of freedom. She knew it was the last time any of her clothes would hang next to his. She packed their clothes in separate boxes and marked them accordingly.

When the clothes were all sorted, marked and packed, she then went back through the bedrooms. She took the pictures off the walls packed the ones she wanted, and left the rest in an open box.

The living room and dining room went quickly. There was not much there on the walls to pack. She never touched anything in the bathrooms. The walls had just been freshly papered.

When Tom came home from work that night he was really pleased with Dawn for all the work she did that day. "Yes," he thought to himself, "having her paint everything would keep her good and busy for the two weeks the children were gone." He even liked the way she marked all the boxes. Everything was stacked in the sunroom by the size of the box, not by name or the room it came from. He didn't know Dawn had a reason for doing it that way.

Chapter 4

It was a beautiful warm, sunny day with a slight breeze. The inmates were busy getting the last preparations ready for the arts and crafts show. In an hour the gates would be open and the "free men" as the inmates called them, would be coming in for the two-day affair. The art show always drew a crowd, which "oohed" and "aahed" at the talent of the inmates.

The inmates had chosen their finest crafts for display. Beautiful paintings of wildlife; fine handmade leather purses, wallets, and clothes; wooden articles such as pictures, wood burnings, and handmade furniture were just a few of the crafts.

Aromas of freshly baked goods filled the air. Homemade fudge, saltwater taffy, hard candy, along with fresh produce was for sale.

Cheers could be heard from the grandstand. In the arena, inmates and civilians were taking their turns riding the bucking bronco. Riders would mount the horse, the gate would open, in a flash the horse would start its bucking and turning, within seconds the rider would be thrown off. It appeared that the horse was the head of this game.

Only the most trusted inmates were allowed to participate at the arts and crafts show. Dakota and Chew were among these known as "Trustees."

By the end of the second day of the show, Dakota had sold all of his crafts. "I can't believe how some of the 'free men' fight over our stuff," he said to Chew.

"Yea, but ain't it great, we sure do make a killing on it though." Dakota smiled, "Sure beats the four cents an hour we make working for the state."

With the show over and everyone leaving, the clean up started. It had been a good year for the prison show. The warden was pleased, as the rodeo was a great way to create good public relations with the civilians.

Sitting in the living room, watching T.V., the phone rang. Chew answered the phone. "Just a minute," he said. "Dakota, it's for you, the warden." Handing the phone over, Dakota answered, "Yea Warden, it's Dakota, what can I do for you, Sir?"

"Could you come down to my office? We need to talk. I have a problem."

"Yes sir, I'll be right down." He hung up the phone.

Thirty minutes later in the wardens' office, "Sit down Dakota." After Dakota sat down the Warden continued, "I was wondering if you could do me a favor?"

"If I can, Warden. All you have to do is ask. What ya got on your mind, Sir?"

"Well, it seems we have a problem on B block, I was wondering if you would mind staying there for a few days and checking it out, the inmates are in an uproar."

"Sure what's the problem?" Dakota asked.

Smiling the warden said, "Well that's what I need you to find out."

Many times, Dakota would be asked to solve a "problem" within the prison population. It would be a "favor" of sorts and "off the record." A problem between inmates was a common occurrence.

On B block Dakota followed the guard down the catwalk, to his cell. Dakota's cell would be 243. The other inmates just looked as he walked by their cells. No one said a word. It was so quite you could have heard a pin drop.

In his cell that night after lights were out Dakota could hear the inmates whispering and spreading the word of his arrival on the block. "Dakota's on the block," he could hear them say.

It didn't take Dakota long to figure out what the problem was. He was sick to his stomach with it. It was enough to gag a maggot.

About three in the morning, Dakota got up off his bunk and

walked to his cell door, it was unlocked. He walked out of it and down the catwalk, five cells down. He pulled on that cell door, and not being surprised, it was also unlocked he walked in. He found three inmates who were sound asleep on their bunks.

Dakota grabbed the inmate on the top bunk and threw him across the room. He then grabbed the next two.

"Jesus!" one of the inmates hollered.

"Not quite, you stinking pig, but your sure gonna wish that I was," Dakota hissed. As Dakota was beating the three of them he hollered at them, "I could be home in my own bed, but no I'm here, on this damn block with pigs who smell worse than any skunk I've ever smelled. Clean is a new word you're going to learn and remember." With that he threw then out on the catwalk and said, "Walk you sorry fuckers. To the shower I'll show you what clean is!"

Ten minutes later Dakota had the three inmates tied up in the shower and was scrubbing them with a long handled wire brush. The more they screamed and begged him to stop, the harder he scrubbed them. When fifteen minutes of this had passed, the guards decided they'd better check to make sure Dakota wasn't killing them.

They walked in and saw the inmates tied up, "What's going on here?" startled, they asked.

Dakota answered, "Only 3 inmates playing scrub a dub in the tub. Right boys?" The three knew they'd better agree with Dakota. Rumor had it if you messed with him, you might live to regret it.

"Yea." That's all they could say.

"OK, I think they've got the idea, Dakota, we'll take it from here," one of the guards said. Smiling, Dakota left the room.

The guards then cut down the three inmates, their bodies were bleeding from head to toe, from the wire brush that Dakota had "showered" them with.

"You boys are lucky he even left any meat on you." The

guards laughed. "Dakota doesn't take kindly to stinking animals. If you're smart you won't forget it."

Chapter 5

As the phone was ringing on the other end, Dawn hoped they could help her. "Good Afternoon, this is U-Haul, Bob speaking, how can I help you?"

"Yes, I would like to know if I could make an appointment to have a Reese hitch put on my van. I also need to rent a U-Haul one way please," Dawn said.

"What day would you like to do this Ma'am?" asked Bob.

"Next Monday afternoon, if possible," replied Dawn.

"Let's see here, I could fit you in at one in the afternoon. How would that be?"

Knowing that wouldn't do because Tom didn't leave for work until two-thirty in the afternoon, Dawn asked, "Do you have anything any later?"

"How about three?" Bob asked.

"That would be just fine," Dawn said with relief.

"Well I just need to get a little information from you. Now do you want to have the hitch welded on or just bolted on?"

"What's the difference?" Dawn asked.

"If you ever sell your van, you could take it back off if it's bolted on. If you have it welded on, it'll never come off. Myself," he went on to say, "I believe the welded ones are stronger."

Hearing this, a quick vision went through Dawns mind. She was traveling down the road with a bolted hitch on, a trailer in tow, the bolts break, the hitch comes off, she and the children are stuck on the side of the road. Realizing that Dawn has left him, Tom goes in search of her, finds her on the side of the road, pulls out a gun and kills her on the spot.

Shuddering, she says, "Then I'd like to have it welded on please." With that all the arrangements were made.

For the rest of the week Dawn would sleep as much as she

22

could during the afternoon and evening. She was so afraid that she would talk in her sleep and Tom would learn of her plans. Finally, the weekend arrived. With only two more days until freedom, Dawn wondered if her heart could stand the strain.

On Saturday Tom shocked Dawn by telling her they were going out to eat and then to a movie. They hadn't done that in years. She wondered what had come over him, but agreed saying it sounded like fun.

They had a nice dinner and went to see the movie "Ghost." It was a real tear jerkier for Dawn. Tom was acting like the man he used to be years ago. She wondered if he was changing back to that man. He was very sweet, romantic, and catered to her in every way he could.

That night when they went to bed Tom even rubbed her back, held her close, kissed her gently good night, and never even mentioned sex. It was like she had stepped back into another time.

She could tell by his deep breathing that Tom was fast asleep. *"Was she going mad?"* she asked herself. Maybe he really was changing. Could it be he really was sorry and knew of all the hurt he had put her through? Was she making a big mistake?

By Sunday morning, Dawn had decided she would stay. She'd call U-Haul in the morning and cancel the appointments.

When Tom got up Sunday morning, he was in a great mood. Dawn was making his breakfast. Tom went over hugged and kissed Dawn like they were newlyweds. While Dawn was pouring Tom's coffee, she was happily daydreaming about them. She added his sugar, served him the coffee. He reached up pulled her on his lap, told her how much he loved her and kissed her gently before he let her up. She was in love again. She went back to the stove to finish breakfast.

Within seconds, Dawn screamed, as hot liquid ran down her back. Tom was yelling at her, "Can't you even make a decent cup of coffee? You know I don't like that much sugar!" When she turned around, Tom hit her in the face with his fist, knocking her out cold.

When Dawn woke up, she heard Tom say, "Lay still, I've got ice on your back, looks like a pretty bad burn." She realized Tom had taken her shirt off and had laid her on the bed. "Honey, I keep telling you that you make that coffee way too hot, now look you went and got yourself burned." Feeling the pain of the burn, Dawn could say nothing to Tom.

Later that evening, Dawn walked out into the back yard. She couldn't believe her eyes. She blinked and looked again. They were still there. Doves, at least 100 of them, all sitting up on the telephone wire that stretched across the back yard. Dawn knew the dove was the Lord's bird and they were all looking at her! Never had Dawn seen so many doves in her life. Tears welled up into her eyes, and she started to cry. The Lord had answered her prayer. He had sent the doves to tell her it was all right to leave Tom. The message was clear.

Monday was here and Dawn felt as though she couldn't breathe. She felt like she was going to jump out of her skin. Her back was still burning from the coffee Tom had poured down her back. This was it, freedom was only hours away.

Tom was getting ready for work. He'd be leaving any minute now. Dawn's heart was pounding so hard it felt like it was going to explode.

"Don't forget you're going to bring me supper tonight. I'll expect you by 6:00," Tom said to Dawn.

"I won't. I've got all your favorites in mind for you tonight," Dawn said. Tom smiled gave her a kiss and out the door he went.

She was so scared! Could she pull this off and get away? What if Tom forgot something and came home, she'd be caught! Better yet did he suspect what she was up to? *"Stop it,"* she told herself. *"Pull yourself together, you've got things to do."*

She took the children over to the neighbors'. She had asked

them a few days earlier if they would watch them while she ran a few errands.

On her way to the U-Haul store, Dawn stopped at the bank and withdrew $700 from their savings account. She also stopped for gas and picked up her first pack of cigarettes. She had never smoked before, but her nerves where shot. She thought this might relax her. Dawn knew cigarette smoking was bad for her health, but she figured living with Tom was bad for her health also. In fact it could be deadly!

With the Reese hitch installed, and the trailer hooked up, Dawn was soon on her way home. Backing up to the house was a little bit more than Dawn had planned on. The trailer went every which direction but the one Dawn wanted it to go. So when all else failed, she just drove it up on the lawn. *"Tom would have a cow if he could see this now,"* Dawn said to herself. She didn't dare laugh now, she thought, *"Maybe, once I'm out of here."*

The packing of the van and trailer went smoothly, thanks to Dawn marking the boxes, Tom's boxes were left in the sunroom, when it was completed Dawn went over to the neighbors' to pick up the children. The neighbors were surprised when Dawn told them she was leaving and wouldn't be back. They didn't ask where she was going and said they didn't want to know. They wouldn't have to lie to Tom that way. Dawn asked them to tell Tom, if he asked, that they never saw her leave. They agreed to this story, as they had the feeling that Tom had been very abusive towards Dawn.

"I just want to thank you for everything," Dawn said. "It's been nice knowing you, maybe when things cool off a bit I'll get in touch with you. We've got to get going now, before Tom wonders where we are. I was supposed to take him supper tonight."

"Why don't you call him and tell him it will be a little late, that way it will give you a little more time?" Sue asked her.

"He will blow his cool at me," Dawn said.

"So let him blow, he can't hurt you over the phone and you won't be there for him to beat, when he does get home." Sue looked at her and grinned.

"That's not a bad idea. He may blow, but this way he won't call and wonder where I am. He'll be expecting me to be late and won't come looking for me. I think I'll do just that," Dawn said.

They all said their good-byes to each other and then Dawn and the children went back to their house.

Dawn made the call, and true to form Tom was hot. "What the hell do you mean your going to be late? You know damn good and well what time I expect my supper!"

"One of the kids must have turned the oven off by mistake, I'm sorry it will be about another half hour." Dawn hated lying and blaming one of the kids, but with Tom if one of the kids did something wrong, it didn't bother him. Dawn didn't want Tom to have any reason to come home, so she used the kids as an excuse.

It worked, he calmed down and said, "Well hurry up and keep a better eye on them. You know I don't like them in the kitchen while you're cooking." With that he hung up.

"Everyone go to the bathroom now and hurry, I'll grab the puppy and we can get going."

"Mom where are we going?" Leigh asked.

"We're going camping for awhile, just us, not Dad, he can't go because he has to work." She wasn't really lying, that's just what they were going to do, hide out in a campground until Dawn could think of something else.

There was a full moon out and the stars were bright. The darkness, with the warm summer air had Dawn relaxing, just a little. It was quite in the van, except for the radio. The children were sleeping, as they always did on a trip.

After two hours on the road, Dawn started to get tired. She could see motel billboards in the distance. She thought they would stop and get a room. She could use a nice relaxing hot bath. The children would sleep better in a bed and wouldn't be cranky in the morning if they did. It would be a long day tomorrow and everyone would need the rest.

When the exit for the motel came Dawn pulled off the highway. She followed the signs to the motel. When she stopped the van, the kids woke up and asked if they were at the campground yet. "No, not yet, tomorrow we'll be there, tonight we're going to stay at this nice motel."

As Dawn and the children walked into the motel lobby, they looked like a mother hen and her chicks following, the motel clerk thought and just smiled.

Once the children were settled in their beds, Dawn ran a hot bath in the tub. "This will feel like heaven," Dawn thought.

As she lowered herself into the warmth of the tub and relaxed, Dawn could hear the children breathing deeply and knew they were content.

They are so excited about the camping trip, sure wish I could feel the same way. I need to find a job, and a real place for us to live. "Lord what am I going to do with four children on my own?" After her bath she went to bed, relaxing she fell asleep hoping to have nice dreams.

A couple hours later Dawn was in a deep sleep when the door crashed open, she sat up in bed and screamed, hearing their mother scream startled the four children. "Daddy, you scared us," one of them said. Dawn panicked, jumped off the bed, but she was too late. Tom grabbed her, through her against the wall, and she hit the floor. Tom jumped on Dawn and straddled her. He took both her hands with one of his and put them above her head, pining her down. The children were screaming, "Daddy, don't hurt Mommy!"

"Get back over on your beds!" he yelled at them. Dawn was struggling to get free, but Tom had the strength of an ox, he controlled Dawn as if she were a rag doll. With Tom's free hand, he reached into his pocket and pulled out a switchblade. He opened it. Dawn's eyes were wide with horror! "You stupid woman, I told you if you ever tried to leave me, I would find you and kill you. Did you really think I wouldn't come looking for you, once I had seen you were gone? Those are my kids, and no one will ever take them from me." Then it happened. Tom plunged the knife into Dawn's throat. She could feel pain, and the warmth of the blood dripping down her neck, the room started spinning. As the darkness slowly started to creep in, she knew she was dying!

The people in the next room heard all the commotion. The man called down to the front desk and told the clerk. "Some guy next door is beating his wife and children are screaming. I paid for a good night's sleep. Now do something about this!" "Yes Sir. What room is the noise coming from?" the clerk asked. "Room 29!" the man said as he hung up the phone. The clerk called the police and explained the situation.

Ten minutes later the police entered the room and found Dawn. Her clothes and hair soaked in her own blood. Tom was still standing over her, screaming at her, demanding that she answer him. The children were all huddled in a corner of the room hugging each other and crying. "Put your hands up, drop the knife or we'll shoot," yelled an officer.

Tom looked at the officer and said, "My wife has hurt herself, she's bleeding, help her!" Tom dropped the knife and stood up. The officers rushed him; handcuffed him and took him out of the room. A lady officer went over to the corner where the children were, bent down and softly spoke to them.

The rescue team rushed in. When they took Dawn's vitals they found none. "It's too late, she's gone," they whispered. They took a blanket off the bed and completely covered Dawn up.

When the day of the funeral came, Dawn's family and friends were there. People from all over had sent beautiful flowers and cards. Everyone seemed so sad. Dawn could hear people talking about Tom. "He'll get life in prison, is what they say." Another voice said, "Well I think they should give him the death penalty." Not caring to listen to this Dawn looked for her children.

She found them. Sitting on a couch, just the four of them, looking so sad. Their eyes were all red from crying. How lost they looked. She just wanted to hug them and tell them it would be all right that, "Mommy was here." But she couldn't she was dead.

At the end of the funeral, the children stood up, walked over to the casket. With tears in their eyes and their voices cracking, they told their mom how much they loved her, as they laid a red rose in her hand.

When they walked away, the attendant started to close the lid to the casket for the last time. Dawn felt as though she were suffocating, and she screamed, "No........no.......I can't be dead!"

"Mom, Mom, MOM...........Wake Up!" Lynn was shaking her. "Mom are you all right?"

Dawn's eyes opened and then she blinked. Was Lynn really standing there? Lynn had her nightgown on. Dawn blinked at her again.

"Lynn is that you, are you really here?" she asked.

"Mom you were having a bad dream. Mom, are you ok?" Lynn asked. Dawn let out a big breath, "Yes honey, I'm ok. I was just having a nightmare." Dawn got up, tucked Lynn back in bed, gave her a quick kiss, and sat down to smoke a badly needed cigarette.

Dawn couldn't sleep the rest of the night. Her nerves were shot. She just sat and watched the door, expecting Tom at any moment.

Chapter 6

It had been a long, hot day working with the dogs. Dakota was bushed. *"A cold beer would taste good about now,"* he thought. *"Guess a Coke will have to do, that is until they start putting bars in prison,"* he laughed at himself, *"and not the kind that go up and down."*

As Dakota was sitting out on the porch, enjoying the cool breeze of the evening, he reached for the phone and dialed the number he knew so well. The phone on the other end was ringing and then his mother's voice answered, "Hello."

"Hey, what's new up north?" Dakota asked. "Oh! Dakota, I'm so glad you called. It always makes my day to talk to you," his Mom said. "That's why I call, Mom. I love putting a smile on your face," he said. With a smile in her voice she said, "Dakota, I'm glad you called now. We plan on being out of town for about a week or so and I didn't want you to worry."

"Oh yea, where are you two young kids going, on a honeymoon or something? A few years too late for that wouldn't you say," he teased his mom.

"Now that's not a bad idea. Just so you know, Mr. Smarty pants, older doesn't mean it's over. It's just getting perfected." She laughed.

"Yes Ma'am, I'll remember that for when I get older. Got any tips I should I write down in my book?" They both laughed. "Ok, so really, where are you going?" he asked.

"You remember me telling you about our friends Marie and Merle? Well, we're going to house sit and stay with their two teenagers for a couple of weeks. They are going to Florida to visit Merle's brother. It'll be closer to work for us and they won't have to worry about the kids while they're gone."

"I guess you won't be bored then will you? Not with two teenagers in the house," he said.

"They're really nice kids, a boy and a girl. We really enjoy them. So what have you been up too lately?" she asked.

"Oh not much really. The President called and wanted to know my thoughts on security for the secret service. Just to see if I had any new ideas, you know. Other than that I've been busy with training the dogs and doing some of my hobby craft."

Laughing she answered, "Really, and what did you tell him?"

"I told him don't call me. I'll call you when I come up with something. I mean, after all, what do they expect when they pay inmates $.04 an hour?" He laughed. Then changing back to a serious tone he said, "All joking aside, I've been working on a really nice coffee table. I've put a lot of hand carving on the top of it. I've made a scene with mountains and even have a few eagles flying through the air. I'll send you a picture of it when I'm done."

"Sounds wonderful! I guess we should get off the phone for now. We're getting ready to leave for Marie's. Let me give you her number. I also wrote you a letter and sent it to you, just in case I didn't talk to you before we left," she said.

"That's my Mom always looking out for her children," he said teasing her.

"Yes I do, and aren't you glad I do?" she said. She gave Dakota Marie's phone number and then they said their good-byes.

Dakota's wasn't an easy life; he was always on the move. He never knew where the agency would need him next. It could be in the U.S. or overseas, depending on which one of his skills they would need.

A few days later Dakota received a phone call from the agency. "Washington? What's going on there?" Dakota asked.

"There's has been a bomb threat on the Pentagon. We need you to fly there and check it out," the agent on the other end said.

"I have to get a few things together and I'll be on my way. See you soon," Dakota said and hung up the phone.

An hour later Dakota and Buck, his bomb dog, were on a flight to Washington, D.C.

When they landed, CIA agents were there to meet them.

The briefing took about two hours; and the agents had their assignments from Dakota. If there was a bomb, they would find it, but it could take hours. Searching the Pentagon for a bomb would be like looking for a needle in a haystack.

After ten hours of searching, Buck stopped by a counter with a coffee pot on it. He looked at the coffee pot and started to whine. When Dakota looked and pointed at the coffee pot without touching it, he said, "What is it boy, is it in here?" Buck's reply was a few more whines and a soft bark. "Good boy, Buck," Dakota said as he gave the dog a few pats. As Dakota carefully looked all around the coffee pot, Buck sat quietly. As he opened the lid slowly to the water reservoir, Dakota held his breath as he looked in. When he saw the bomb hidden in there, he slowly closed the lid, backed away from the coffee pot and let out the breath he held. Then looking at Buck, Dakota said, "Of all the places to put a bomb, in the coffee pot. Well Mr. Coffee was sure going to make one bang of a pot."

Dakota radioed the bomb squad and gave them his location in the Pentagon. Within a few minutes the bomb was dismantled.

After the debriefing, Dakota and Buck were on their way back to the airport. When they reached the private plane waiting for them, Dakota patted his dog's head and said, "Well boy it's back to prison for us." Buck looked at Dakota and then jumped into the plane. "Your one crazy dog, Buck," Dakota said, smiling at his dog.

Two weeks later as Dakota walked down to his wood shop, Dakota was in deep thought. In his last conversation with the President, Dakota had agreed to fly out to Washington, D.C. and go over his ideas with the "top brass" of the secret service.

Dakota had been working with them on a number of things during the past few years.

But working on the coffee table was pure enjoyment. The eagle had its wings spread wide flying free over the mountains with not a care in the world. The carving had taken many hours, but at long last, was nearly done. *"This is a table I would like in my house someday,"* Dakota thought. He let his mind drift off to someday when he would have a wife and kids, lots of them he thought. His wife would be sweet, understanding, his best friend and would trust him. He in turn would love her always and would protect her at all cost. Someday I'll find her and it won't matter to her that I've been in prison.

Chapter 7

Pulling into the circle drive at her sister Marie's house was easy. *"Thank goodness, no backing up here,"* Dawn thought. Seeing a strange car, Dawn wondered who is here.

As they entered the house, her niece and nephew came running to great them. "Aunt Dawn," they said. Hugging them and looking over their shoulders, Dawn noticed a couple she had never seen before. Her niece and nephew then introduced her and the children to Cheryl and Rick. "Hello," they all said to each other. Irene and Kevin then wanted to know if they could take their cousins, Lynn, Leigh, Louise, and Scott out to the pool for a swim. "Sure, why not?" Dawn said. The children quickly changed into their swimsuits and were out the door.

"Want a cup of coffee?" Cheryl asked Dawn.

"Yes, that would be nice, thank you. Where are Marie and Merle?"

"Oh I thought Marie told you. She was going to go to Florida and asked us to stay with Kevin and Irene," Cheryl said.

"You're right, she did. It must have slipped my mind." Dawn was wondering if Marie had told Cheryl she would be storing things in the pole barn.

"Marie had asked us if we would mind helping you put your things in the pole barn. I hope you don't mind, but Marie kinda filled us in on what was going on." Cheryl went on, "Your sister and I have been good friends for many years. You don't have to worry. We won't tell a soul."

Dawn smiled, "Marie has talked a lot about you too, I kinda feel like I know you already. I'm not worried, and thanks for helping."

"No problem, everyone has an x-asshole somewhere. Honey you're not the first, and I'm sad to say, won't be the last,"

Cheryl said with a big smile.

The U-Haul was emptied in no time at all. Dawn thanked Cheryl and Rick for all their help and was getting ready to leave when Cheryl asked, "Why don't you and the children come back tomorrow night for supper. We'd sure enjoy the company."

"Thank you I'd like that, what can I bring?" Dawn asked.

"Nothing, we have enough here to feed an army. You just worry about getting settled at the campground and leave the rest up to us," Cheryl said. With that Dawn and the children left. She returned the U-Haul, and headed for her dad's to get her pop-up. He had borrowed it from her last summer. It was stored at the back of his property. He would be gone at this time of day and would never miss it.

As Dawn checked in at the office of the campground and paid for a month of camping she went back to the van, and said to her children, "Now our fun begins." The children were all excited.

Once at the campsite, Dawn and the children began setting up camp. The pop-up was old and soon Dawn discovered the canvas was pretty much shot. But up went the tents, and the van was soon emptied. With everything settled in, they all took a walk to the camp store to buy a plastic tarp for the pop-up.

The children were laughing at Dawn as she put the tarp over the camper; they said it looked like a circus tent. Standing back looking at it herself, Dawn agreed it did, she laughed and started chasing the children around the campsite, saying, "We should live in a circus tent. Look at the little clowns I live with."

"Mom, can we walk around the campground?" Leigh asked.

"Sure, let's all go and see what the bath house and pool look like," Scott said.

"Why not, lets go, we're on vacation, but we'd better wake up sleepy head first," Dawn told them. Louise, her youngest, was sleeping in the van. Dawn woke her up and said, "Louise,

I swear you were born tired. Come on sleepy we're going for a walk." Louise always woke up happy and just bounced out of the van.

The water from the pool sparkled from the sunlight. It was the prettiest blue Dawn had seen in a long time. The water slide curved as it came down to the pool. The loungers were plentiful.

The pool house was large. Inside there were plenty of showers, dressing rooms, hair and body dryers. Seven stalls with plenty of sinks and mirrors. "Mom, we won't have to take turns to go to the bathroom, we can all go at the same time. Heck we can even have a race to see who gets done the fastest," said Louise. They all laughed.

"You think you'd win? Everyone knows a boy can go faster than girls," Scott said proudly.

"That's not true! Mom, tell him that's not true!" Louise said.

"Let's have a race right now and find out," said Lynn. Before Dawn knew what was happening each child stood in front of a stall.

"Ok Mom, count down," said Leigh.

Laughing at them, Dawn counted down, "On your marks, get ready, set, go!" In the stalls they all rushed, it wasn't long and the toilets were flushing, out flew her four children.

"It's a tie," Louise said. Everyone was laughing.

"Now that I know I have the fastest flushers in the world, let's go see the rest of the camp," Dawn said, smiling.

The campground was nestled in the woods. Large oaks, maples, elms, and birch trees were throughout the camp. Every campsite had water, electricity, a grill, and a nice fire pit. As they walked around the camp, other campers would say, "Hello."

"Supper was delicious, Cheryl. Thank you for asking us."

"It was nothing. I'm really glad you came. Let's go sit out by the pool with our coffee and visit while the kids swim,"

Cheryl said.

Out by the pool they sat down and started to visit. "How old are your children?"

"Lynn is the oldest, she's 10, and Leigh's 8, Scott's 6 and Louise is 5," Dawn said.

"They're sure cute, and so well behaved," Cheryl said.

"How many children do you have?"

Cheryl laughed, "Five, my oldest two are girls, and then I have three boys." Cheryl appeared to be about her mother's age, Dawn asked.

"Do they all live around here?"

"My youngest two boys live on the other side of the state, my daughters live about an hour from here, and my oldest son lives down south. He's in prison."

"For what?" Dawn asked.

"Oh, they say he killed someone. He's in there for murder. But I know it's not true," Cheryl said. "Let me tell you about Dakota."

As Dawn listened to Cheryl tell the story about Dakota and what had happened twelve years ago, she knew it sounded familiar.

"I've heard a story like this from a friend of mine before, and I use to know a Dakota, back when I was younger. Your son's name isn't Dakota Deer is it?"

"Why yes it is, how did you know Dakota?" Cheryl asked.

"Oh, as teenagers we all use to hang out at the roller rink, Dakota was one of the best skaters I'd ever seen. Girls use to fall all over him. Dakota was hot. I never dated him, but we were friends. He just wasn't my type, too wild back then. I was kinda square, the down to earth type. I bet I was the only girl within miles that wasn't throwing herself at him. Maybe that's why we were just friends."

Cheryl laughed. "That sure sounds like Dakota. I think he had girlfriends in every town. If the phone rang in the evening, we knew it must be for Dakota. It got to the point I quit answering the phone and just let him get it."

"A friend of mine told me he got life, is that true?" Dawn asked.

"Yes that's what they say, but we're working on getting him out. He'll be out someday." Cheryl went on, "You see he works at the Dog Pen and has gotten to know several senators and important people through his woodworking. I have a video of him. Would you like to see it?"

"You have a video of him in prison?" Dawn asked.

"Yes, but you won't think he's in prison once you see it. I can only be thankful Dakota's where he is and not locked up in a cell. Come on in. I'll put it in the VCR for you."

As they watched the video together, Dawn was amazed. Dakota had grown up; he was dark skinned, due to being part Indian. His hair was a deep brown, medium length, and feathered back. His bedroom eyes were deep blue; his wonderful smile could make a woman's heart melt. It was apparent that he worked out as his chest and arms were very muscular. He spoke in the video with a very sexy southern accent.

Dakota was showing his private woodshop where he had all his own tools. The furniture he was building, wood burned pictures he had done, and even some rings he had made.

Dawn looked at Cheryl, "He does this in prison? How can that be?"

"Oh it gets better, wait till you see the rest of it", Cheryl said proudly. As Dakota walked out of his woodshop, the camera followed him to the outside of his ranch house. As he walked throughout the yard, the view was beautiful. In the background the barn could be seen, with several horses in the corral. Next Dakota walked over by the dog pens and explained what kind of dogs they were and what they were trained for. The location looked just like anyone's ranch anywhere. *"Where were the tall fences and the guards?"* thought Dawn. Dakota's voice brought her back from her thoughts. He was walking around talking about the ranch as if he owned the place. When the video ended, Dawn looked at Cheryl with a thousand questions on her mind. Cheryl smiled, "Come on I'll explain it to you over coffee."

Chapter 8

In the woods about thirty feet up in a tree, Dakota was dressed in camouflage. Not a soul knew he was there. Quietly he watched them through his binoculars. The children he noticed were having a good time in the pool. The two teenagers, who must be Kevin and Irene, kept a good eye on the four small ones, he thought. Then his eye caught a movement. He moved the binoculars over to focus in. His mom was with a younger lady. Dakota noticed the younger woman's long, blond hair. As they stepped onto the deck and sat down in the chairs, Dakota noticed the blond was small and about his age. And he thought to himself, "I know this lady from somewhere, but where?" He watched them all evening and couldn't get the blond off his mind.

Dusk approached and Dawn called out to her children. "Come on fish, out of the pool. You must be water logged by now. We've got to get back; the sandman's waiting."

Dakota slipped down the tree, through the woods and out to his car, his movements undetected. He was going to find out who she was.

Dawn and the children thanked Cheryl for supper and were on their way. Dakota followed her at a distance. As Dawn pulled into the campground, Dakota drove right by. He found the next dirt road and turned there. He parked his car in a field of corn, to hide it, and then walked through the woods towards the campground.

At the bathhouse the children quickly brushed their teeth, went to the bathroom, and headed back to the campsite. Dawn was building a fire for them.

"Are we roasting marshmallows tonight?" asked Scott.

"We can if you want to. I thought maybe we'd sit around and tell stories, also."

"Oh Mom, not stories about when you were a kid again," said Lynn.

"Yea Mom, tell us some ghost stories," Leigh pleaded.

"Ok, you win, ghost stories it is," Dawn smiled.

When they were done roasting their marshmallows and had their seats around the campfire, Dawn started to tell them a ghost story.

Quiet as a mouse, Dakota was up the tree watching and listening to Dawn and her children. As Dawn told the ghost story, Dakota smiled to himself. Dawn was getting to a scary part; the children were on the edge of their seats. Crack, a sound came from behind the children, they all jumped up from their seats. They looked behind them, as if expecting, a big ghost to come out and get them. *"Sound effect is the only way to go with a ghost story,"* Dakota thought. Pleased with the reaction of the children Dakota sat and watched.

"Mom, that was a really good story. Tell us another one," Louise asked.

"Not tonight, it's late and you monsters need to get to bed. Come on I'll tuck you in." As Dawn tucked each one of her children in, she kissed them good night, and told them to have sweet dreams.

Sitting back out by the campfire, Dawn let her mind drift off to the video with Dakota in it. Those blue eyes, and that smile of his. It was almost as if he were looking at her. What was he trying to tell her? Something told her she needed to talk to this man. He had answers and lots of them. "This is ridiculous, I haven't seen Dakota Deer in years. What could he possibly do for me? Wake up, Dawn, the man's in prison. You might as well be telling yourself Patrick Swazey's going to walk into your life and make everything all better." With this she laughed at herself, got up stirred the coals, walked to her tent and got ready for bed.

Dakota heard Dawn talking to herself, *"So we do know each other. I need to find out more about you. A phone call to mom will answer some questions,"* he thought. Dakota then left the camp ground and returned to his car. Picking up his cell phone he dialed Marie's number.

"Hello," Cheryl said.

"Hey, what's new up in God's country? How's the baby sitting going?"

"They're not babies, Dakota, they're very nice teenagers. Everything's going just fine. You'll never guess who I ran into. Someone you know," Cheryl said teasing.

"Oh really, like who, the pope?" he teased back.

"No silly, someone you use to know years ago. Her name is Dawn Brown, she use to be Dawn Star. She married Tom Brown. You might remember him. Anyway, she is Marie's youngest sister. She's left her husband and getting a divorce. Guess the guy's a real jerk, beat her all the time."

"So do they have children?" Like he really needed an answer to that, but thought he'd better ask.

"Yes, four of them. Dakota, they are so well behaved. And they all are as cute as a button. Do you remember Dawn?" she paused.

"I knew, I knew her, Dawn Star," he thought to himself. "Yea, I remember her, kinda square, the quiet type, but a friend. I tried to get her to go out with me once, but her mom said no. Guess it was lucky for Dawn she didn't go, or one of those kids might have been mine."

"Anyway, she's a real sweet girl. I really feel sorry for her, with four kids and alone. Do you know where she's staying with them now?" Before he could answer, she went on. "In a campground. She doesn't want anyone to know where she is. That girl is scared to death of her husband. She hasn't even told her family, other than Marie, where she is."

Dakota didn't like the sounds of that. A woman scared enough to hide out with children, even from her own family. He had seen cases like this before. "Ma, you make it sound like she fears for her and the children's lives."

"I don't think for the children. She says Tom would never harm a hair on their heads, but he has beaten her badly in front of them. She claims he'll kill her if he finds her."

"Do you think she's telling the truth? What if she's just making it up, ya know, to make you feel sorry for her?" Dakota asked.

"Not a chance, Dakota, She's telling the truth. She has that look of fear in her eye," Cheryl said.

"Well, Ma, I hope she's going to be ok. Help her if you can. She's going to need all the friends she can get right now, ones she can trust."

"I will, Dakota. Well, guess we should go for now. Call me again in a few days. I'll let you know what's going on," Cheryl said.

"Ok, Mom. You take care. I love you."

"I love you too, Dakota," she said. As they both hung up their phones.

Dakota picked up the phone again. "Good evening CIA, Agent Smith. How can I help you?" the woman said.

"Yea, this is Special Agent Deer. I need a background check run on a Thomas Brown, I believe he was born in the mid to late 50's. I need this ASAP."

"Where do you want it sent, agent Deer?"

"Fax it to my car, Agent Smith. I'll be waiting."

"Yes sir, it'll be about 10 minutes, good-bye, Agent Deer."

Dakota lit up a cigarette and sipped on his coke. His thoughts drifted back to another time. The music was loud and the roller skaters were having a good time. The announcer's voice came over the P.A. "The next skate is for couples only." As the lights dimmed down and the soft music started Dakota skated over to the shy little blond. "So, do you want to skate?" he asked.

She looked up at him from her seat. "Sure, I'd like that." Dakota took Dawn's hand in his and they skated out to the rink floor. As they skated around the rink floor, Dakota slipped his arm around Dawn's waist, still hanging onto her other hand. "I never see you at any of the parties Dawn, how come?" he teased.

"Dakota, you know I'm just not into any of that. I've told you before, I won't knock you for what you do, if you don't knock me for not doing it."

"Yea, but you could still go. No one's going to make you drink or smoke pot," Dakota said. Dawn's stern look at him gave Dakota her answer. "Ok, you win, I won't try to talk you into it, but I sure would like to see you," he said.

Dawn laughed, "Dakota, you know I'm not like the girls you date. Besides, if we dated it would ruin our friendship. I don't plan on being one of those girls you love and leave."

"Come on, Dawn, you make me sound bad. I've never made anyone any promises. I never tell any of them that I love them," Dakota said.

"Maybe not, Dakota, but you know they think you do and I'm not up to getting my heart broken," she said.

"Dawn, you're a special girl," he said as he tightened his arm around her.

Dakota respected Dawn for her honesty. She was pure at heart and special. The kind of girl a guy would want for a wife when he got ready to settle down.

The buzzing of the fax machine drew Dakota back to the present. He started to read it: Thomas A. Brown, born 1955. Arrested several times for assault and battery on women. Charges dropped by victim. Arrested for rape. Charges dropped by victim. As he continued down the list, there were several speeding tickets, and a few DWI's. Court ordered AA. Tom had been arrested and convicted for possession of marijuana, and served 6 months in county jail. Married divorcee Dawn Jones, maiden name Star, in 1981.

Dakota could only imagine the real reason the victims would drop the charges. It just didn't seem fair that a guy like this could get "off" all the time. *"This man,"* Dakota thought, *"needs to be in prison. "*

Dakota's phone was ringing, "Hello," he said.

"This is Agent Smith, did the fax come through?"

"Yes, thank you, Agent Smith," Dakota said.

"Is there anything else you need, Agent Deer?" she asked.

Following his gut instinct and his heart from years ago, Dakota said, "Yes, I need you to put me through to Colonel Williams."

"Right away Agent Deer," she said as she transferred the call.

"Colonel Williams here," the man said.

"Agent Deer Sir. I need a surveillance/security team. Code 777."

"Where do you want them?" Williams asked.

"In Michigan, to follow and observe Dawn Brown, and her children. They are not to approach her. Not unless she is in danger. I want a homing device placed in her car. She is staying at Camp Hide-a-way."

"They will be on their way within the hour," Colonel Williams confirmed.

"Thank you, Sir."

The next morning Dawn called Cheryl from the campground pay phone. "Hello," Cheryl answered.

"Good Morning Cheryl. This is Dawn. I was wondering if you would mind if Irene watched my children today for a while. I'd like to go job hunting and look for a house to rent."

"I think she'd enjoy that. Why don't you bring the children over here? They can swim in the pool. When you're done with your errands and get back I'll make a late lunch," Cheryl said.

"I don't want to put you to all that work." Dawn said.

"It's no problem at all. We'd enjoy the company. Maybe I can even help you with some ideas about where you could find a place to rent."

"Thanks, Cheryl, that would be really great. See you soon."

Dawn noticed, as she went back to the campsite, with her

children that they had new neighbors. A couple of young men had pulled in and started to set up camp. The young men said, "Hello." Dawn smiled and returned the greeting.

With the children in the van they were off to her sister Marie's. She was looking forward to finding a job and hoping to find a house to rent. It was still nice weather; so finding the house could wait for a couple of months.

"Agent Raymond, the subject is on the move. You can pick her up as she leaves the camp ground," Agent Dean said.

"Will do. I see her now. Are you guys getting set up all right?" Agent Raymond asked.

"Yep. This should be a piece of cake right next door to her site," Agent Dean said.

"Don't let Agent Deer hear you kid around like that. He'll have your ass on the chopping block. That man has no sense of humor," Agent Raymond told Dean.

"You're telling me! I don't think Agent Deer even knows what enjoying life is all about. He's so dead serious about everything. Does the man even have a life, or is work the only thing he knows?" asked Agent Dean.

"All I know is the guy is good at what he does, and even the President thinks the world of Agent Deer. The guy is top notch. If Agent Deer wants something done this way or that, no one questions it," Agent Raymond scolded him. "Agent Deer is not a man to fuck with."

"All right, calm down, I get your drift. Agent Dean out."

"Agent Peters, you guys set up?" Agent Raymond called.

"Yep, we're here. She's just now pulling into the drive," Agent Peters answered.

"She plans on leaving the kids there today. So you guys keep an eye on the house. We'll follow her and see what she's up to," Agent Raymond told him.

"Got it," Agent Peters replied.

"Good morning. Would you like a cup of coffee before you go?" asked Cheryl.

"No, I'd better not. I left the van running. I've got a lot of places to go and apply for a job. Morning, they say, is the best time to do this," Dawn said.

"All right, well good luck. We'll have lunch ready about one, does that sound ok to you?"

"That sounds really nice. Cheryl, I can't thank you enough for being so nice to the children and me."

"Dawn, everyone's had problems in their life at one time or another. I believe people should be there to help each other. I've been where you are at one time in my life too." On impulse Dawn quickly gave Cheryl a hug and was out the door.

As Dawn went from one business to another putting in her applications, she felt light at heart and had a good feeling something would work out. When she was driving by the local radio station and saw a sign in the window, "Help Wanted." She stopped in and asked about filling out an application. The secretary gave her one. Dawn filled it out and gave it back to her. Seeing Dawn's past job experiences, she asked Dawn if she would mind staying for an interview. Dawn's heart leaped. She told the secretary she would be more than happy to stay. Dawn sat down in the lobby and waited. The secretary came back and asked Dawn if she would follow her.

"Hello, my name is Jay. I'm the manager of WTLK." He held out his hand and shook Dawn's. "Hello, I'm Dawn Brown. Thank you for taking the time to talk to me," Dawn said.

"I see here on your application that you've had experience in sales before," Jay said.

"Yes sir, I have. I worked in sales at a Lumber Company. I was manager of the siding, windows, and furnace department. My job entailed bookkeeping, time cards, and training employees in sales and marketing," Dawn said smiling.

"I also see that you've been to a business college."

"Yes sir, I spent two years at Masons Business School."

"Well Ms. Brown, let me tell you about the job opening we have here at WTLK. We are looking for an account executive.

The job entails going out to businesses and selling them air time. In other words, selling commercials. You would be writing the commercials and producing them. Before they hit the air, you'd take a tape of the commercial back to the client and get their approval. If the client approves it, it then goes on the air. We call this a non-tangible item. The pay is $8.00 an hour to start, with commission. Do you think this is a job you would like?" Jay asked Dawn.

"Oh yes, thank you," Dawn said.

"Could you start next Monday? Be here about 8:00 am?"

"Yes, I'll be here. Thank you again," Dawn said smiling. They stood up and Jay walked Dawn to the door. "It will be a pleasure having you on our team, Ms. Brown."

"Thank you, Sir. See you Monday." With that Dawn was out the door.

Driving downtown to the grocery store. Dawn went to the bakery department and picked up two homemade strawberry-rhubarb pies. Then it was to the frozen food section for vanilla ice cream. At the checkout Dawn picked up the local newspaper.

On the drive back to Marie's house, Dawn was very excited. *"I've got a job now and soon we'll have a home."* She said to herself.

As she walked into the house Dawn called out, "Hello, I'm back."

"We're out here by the pool," Irene answered.

"Ok. I'll be out in a minute. I've got some things to put away first." Dawn put the ice cream in the freezer and the pies in the refrigerator. She then walked outside by the pool. "Are you fish having a good time?"

"Mom, the water is really warm. Get your suit on and jump on in," Lou said.

"Not now honey, maybe later," Dawn said.

"Dawn, I didn't hear you come in. I was in the family room talking on the phone with Dakota. He says to tell you Hi,"

Cheryl smiled. "How did the job hunting go?"

"I've got a job! I'll be working at the radio station WTLK. I start Monday."

"We'll have coffee, then you can tell me about it," Cheryl said.

Dawn told Cheryl about the job. Cheryl could see Dawn was excited. "Now all I have to do is find us a place to live. I picked up a newspaper today. Thought that would be a good place to start. Oh, Cheryl, I'm sorry in all my excitement I forgot to ask you how Dakota was. You said you were on the phone to him when I came in."

"Oh he's fine. He said to tell you Hello. I hope you don't mind, I've told him about you and the children. It's not like he's going to tell anyone from prison. He really wishes you well. He says he remembers you from when you two were teenagers. He told me you were good friends," Cheryl said.

"No, I don't mind that you told him. I'm not too worried that he'll call up here and tell Tom where I'm at." Dawn laughed. "He really was a good friend back when we were younger. Do you think he'd mind if I wrote to him?" Dawn asked.

"I'll give you his address, but don't be hurt if he doesn't write back. Dakota's not much for writing. And with you going through a divorce, I'm not sure he will at all. He seems to think married women are hands off, but you can give it a whirl." Cheryl smiled. *"He'll write,"* she thought to herself. He really enjoyed hearing from old friends.

That night back at the campground with the children tucked in bed; Dawn was sitting by the campfire. Looking through the newspaper, Dawn found a couple of places to rent. She'd call them in the morning. Next she picked up the phone book she had borrowed from her sister's house. Cheryl had told Dawn to take it since Marie had four of them. She was looking for a divorce lawyer. She wrote down a couple of names and numbers. She would call them this week sometime and file for divorce.

Dawn was getting tired and went to bed. Lying in her bed, Dakota was on her mind. He had told his mom to tell her hello. He would be a safe man to write to. After all he was in prison for life and could never hurt her. Dawn remembered Dakota being a lot of things,' but for him to kill someone just didn't seem possible. Sure he was a Don Juan with the girls in his time, and liked to party, but killing someone? Maybe he got into some really bad drugs. *"That must be it,"* she thought. Maybe when she found time she'd write to him and see how he was doing. She rolled over, closed her eyes, and fell asleep.

Chapter 9

A month later Dakota was in Washington, D.C. in the CIA building, about to conduct a meeting. As the agents sat down the meeting began. "I want to thank you all for coming. In front of you, you each will find a packet containing information of the latest terrorist movements in the United States. Our international airports seem to be the prime targets at this time. As you look in your paperwork, you will see the airports to the east are the main targets, and the overseas flights are hit upon the most. I feel this is only the beginning. I believe the terrorist will soon hit upon our domestic flights as well. For this reason I have notified the FAA of the new security plan to be in place within the month at each and every airport around the country.

"The international airports will have anti-terrorism teams assigned to them to train the local security guards. The details of this training are contained in your packets. Each of you has your assignment in your packets. The training will take about a month.

"Along with this I have ordered tighter security at the boarders and ports of call. I have also assigned teams at each destination for training the security guards there. Each team will be assigned three bomb dogs. The bomb dogs will be left at there given assignment when the training is complete.

"Ladies and gentlemen, our government is spending millions of dollars on this new security plan. The United States will not tolerate terrorism. I have personally gone over this plan with the President. Are there any questions?" Agent Deer asked.

Agent Deer scanned the room. Seeing no one had any questions, he continued. "You will leave for your assignments Monday. Good luck, and if you have any problems or concerns, feel free to contact my office."

As the agents left the room Colonel Williams walked up to Agent Deer. "Agent Deer, may I have a moment of your time?" Looking at Col. Williams Agent Deer replied, "Colonel Williams, how can I help you Sir?"

"No, Agent Deer, Dakota, the question is, how can I help you?"

"Sir?" he asked.

"Dakota, we're alone, and I think we've known each other long enough you can call me Henry, don't you? The question I want to ask you is, how is your assignment going in Michigan?"

"Fine, Sir, just fine." Dakota wasn't about to let his guard down, not even for Colonel Williams.

He was not offended by Agent Deer's reaction because he knew this was what made Agent Deer top notch. Colonel Williams smiled and said, "Good I'm glad to hear it. If you need anything else, give me a call." As he walked away, Colonel Williams turned and said, "By the way Agent Deer, the anti-terrorist plan is a great idea."

"Thank you, Sir," Agent Deer replied.

Alone in the room Dakota sat down. He let his mind wander. "I can protect the President and the country from terrorist. Now, how do I protect that sweet little blond and her four children?"

He heard his other voice answer, "Dakota you're getting too close. Be an agent, not a man with a heart. Treat her like an assignment. You haven't seen her in years; she's nothing to you. An assignment, Dakota."

He answered his other voice, "Yea well she didn't steal your heart years ago. I never even got the chance to show her I really cared. Or that all she had to do was snap her fingers and I would have been hers."

"Protect her now, Dakota. Show her you care later. Be her agent now!" The other voice was firm. Shaking his head, Dakota got up and left the room.

Standing in front of the Lincoln Memorial, Dakota took in a deep breath. He ran up the many stairs in no time flat. At the top Dakota walked into the memorial. The memorial was huge inside and at the back of the room sitting on his giant size chair was Abe Lincoln. Leaning on one of the many pillars, Dakota crossed his arms and scanned the room. In the back of the room there were about thirty small children, the age of sixth graders Dakota guessed, and five adults. A guide was standing in front of Mr. Lincoln telling the group about the past president and the history of the memorial and how it came to be. Dakota noticed the children were in awe of the man sitting on the giant chair. To the right of the room stood a young couple; on the left side of the room stood a man. Dakota looked him over. The man was dressed in blue jeans, a western style shirt, and casual shoes.

The tour guide was now leading her group towards the stairs. As the children and the adults walked by Dakota, he nodded to them. The young couple followed them also.

Dakota walked over and stood in front of Abe Lincoln. Looking up at the statue Dakota noticed the man had walked up next to him. "So how ya been, Harold?" Dakota asked.

"Keeping busy, there's always something to do or see in D.C. Not a dull moment here, How about you?" asked Harold. When Dakota didn't answer, Harold went on. "Ok boy, what's on your mind? You didn't just ask me here for nothing. Something's bothering you."

Harold knew Dakota, not only on a work level, but personally as well. Harold was old enough to be Dakota's father. When Dakota had joined the secret service years ago, Harold was Dakota's first partner. Harold had taken Dakota under his wing, like a father would a son. Harold taught Dakota many things and encouraged him to excel to his fullest potential. Over the years, it was Harold to whom Dakota would always turn.

Dakota turned and looked at Harold. Seeing the look on

Dakota's face and the haze in his eyes, Harold laughed. "So, my boy, the look on your face tells me that heart of steel you have in you is just a little confused. What's the problem, Dakota?"

"It's the past Harold, someone in my past, who I care about. I'm not really sure what to do about it."

Putting his hand on Dakota's shoulder Harold went on, "Could it be Agent Deer, this is something all the training in world isn't going to help you with? Let's go get something to eat and we'll talk about it. So a woman, at long last has touched that cold heart of yours."

Dakota just looked at Harold. *"The man really knows me,"* he thought to himself. "Food is always on your mind Harold," Dakota said.

"Yes it is. So let's go grab a bite and see what we can do about your problem," Harold said smiling.

Sitting at the picnic table at her campsite while the children were at the playground, Dawn was looking at the newspaper for places to rent. Dawn had already called on a few ads in the paper about apartments for rent. She found the landlords wanted $450 a month plus utilities and no pets were allowed. *"This just wouldn't do,"* she thought. As she checked out the rest of the ads, Dawn found one that said: "For rent, possible land contract, two bedroom trailer, garage, fenced in yard, and garden house." Thinking this might be small but they couldn't go on living in a campground, Dawn walked over to the pay phone and called. The lady on the other end agreed to show Dawn the trailer the next day. Writing down the directions, Dawn thanked the lady, who had introduced herself as Kathy.

The next day Kathy was waiting as Dawn and the children pulled into the driveway. She looked to be a woman in her forties. She had a warm smile and was medium in build. "Good morning, I'm Kathy and these must be your children."

"Good morning, I'm Dawn and yes these are my children, Lynn, Leigh, Lou, and Scott."

"Hello," Kathy said to the children. They all said "Hello" back.

Smiling Kathy said, "Come on I'll show you the trailer." They entered the trailer through an enclosed front porch that had been added on, the first room they entered was a cozy living room with the kitchen and dining area to the left. To the right of the living room was a small bedroom. Next they walked through the kitchen to a short hall, off the hall was a small bathroom and a small pantry. Across from the bathroom the back door, exited out to the fenced in back yard. At the end of the hall was another small bedroom. The home was small but cozy and gave Dawn and the children a sense of belonging. As Kathy took them out the back door into the yard they walked over to the garden house. It was made of glass. "This is where I used to start my seedlings for my garden. It's also great for growing herbs. The houseplants in the spring and fall just love it in here," Kathy said. Dawn could see Kathy doing something like this, she was so down to earth.

Next they looked in the garage. It had a tall garage door, Kathy explained that the gentleman who built the garage put in the tall door for them as Kathy and her husband owned a large boat.

"So what do you think?" Kathy asked Dawn.

"I really like it, the neighborhood looks nice and there seems to be children around. That would be nice for my children. How much is the rent?"

"The rent is $250 a month. If you want to buy it after a year, we'll use your first year's rent as a down payment and then sell it to you on a land contract. The sale price is $14,000. Before we sell it on a land contract, we want to rent it for a year. If a person is always on time with their rent we figure they won't have a problem making payments on a land contract. The interest will be 10% if you decide after a year to buy." Dawn couldn't believe what she was hearing! This was an answer to a prayer. "I'll take it today, and I plan on buying!" she exclaimed.

They filled out the paperwork and Dawn gave Kathy the first and last months' rent. Smiling, Kathy gave Dawn the keys to the trailer and said, "Welcome to your new home."

"Thank You," Dawn said.

The next few days were busy for Dawn. She moved all her things from her sisters and had most of it now in her garage.

It seemed to Dawn she had been forever unpacking and putting things away. And the garage was still full of boxes. She was beginning to wonder if it would all fit into this small two bedroom trailer. *"Oh well what won't fit can just stay out there,"* she said to herself. Now the phone was ringing. Dawn walked over and picked it up, "Hello."

"So are we all unpacked and settled yet?" It was her sister Marie."

"Well I think it's as good as it's going to get for today. What are you up to?"

"Nothing much really. Just thought I'd call and check on you and the kids. Are they getting settled in all right? What do they think of the neighborhood?" Marie asked.

"They have kids here to play with. In fact, they are outside now. It seems the kids here really like playing basketball in my driveway. Guess we're the only ones who have a basketball hoop on our garage. I had to move the car on the grass for them. It's really nice, having kids their age for them to play with."

"Well if you need any help with anything just let me know. I won't keep you 'cause I know you're busy. Call me later if you have time," Marie said.

"I will, and thanks for all your help. Bye for now." Dawn hung up the phone.

Chapter 10

Now, a couple months later, Dawn and the children were all settled into a nice family routine. Dawn went to work at the radio station every day, the children were enrolled into school, and the neighbors were friendly and warm.

The divorce was finally over and Dawn received custody of the children. No visitation was allowed for Tom. The judge had reasoned that Tom was a very violent man and was afraid that Tom could turn that violence towards the children. Even though Tom had never harmed any of the children, the judge wasn't about to take any chances.

Cheryl and Dawn's friendship had developed into a mother-daughter relationship. Cheryl treated Dawn's children as grandchildren. The children loved going to Grandma Cheryl's house. She lived in the country where the children had lots of room to roam. Grandma Cheryl also had a hot tub that the children just loved to soak in.

One day while they were out to Cheryl's, she got out pictures of Dakota and showed them to Dawn. The pictures were of Dakota from his younger days until the present time of his being in prison. As they looked at the more recent pictures, Dawn began daydreaming of Dakota.

She wondered what it would be like to talk with him. Maybe even go down south and visit him at the prison. Dawn didn't even hear a word Cheryl was saying.

"Earth to Dawn. Come in Dawn, this is earth," Cheryl said with a laugh.

"Oh, I'm sorry Cheryl. I was just daydreaming," Dawn said sheepishly.

"So I see. How about some more coffee? So what planet were you on?"

"Oh, I was thinking about Dakota. I feel really bad that I

haven't written to him yet. I just haven't had the time. I'm not really sure what to say."

As she poured them some more coffee Cheryl said, "Just tell him about yourself and the children. And what you've been up to all these years. He'd really enjoy that. It doesn't have to be fancy. Just be yourself," Cheryl smiled.

"Yea, I'll get around to it, maybe one evening once the children are in bed. It'll give me something to do."

"Dawn, Dakota's not going to sit in judgment of you if that's what you're worried about. He's not that way. He knows what I had to go through with five children to support and raise on my own," Dawn just smiled at Cheryl.

That evening once Dawn had tucked her children in their beds, she sat in the living room and thought about what to write to Dakota. She got out the paper and pen. *"What do I say, how do I begin?"* Dawn thought to herself. *"Well here goes nothing,"* Dawn thought.

Dear Dakota,

Your mom gave me your address and so I thought I'd write. I'm Dawn Brown but I used to be Dawn Star. I have four children now. My daughters' names are Lynn, Leigh, and Louise, who likes to be called Lou. I also have a son named Scott.

I got married the first time two weeks out of high school. My two oldest children were born during the six years that marriage lasted. My husband was deep into drugs and other women, so I left him. I then married, a man name Tom Brown. You might remember him. He adopted my oldest two children, and then we had two more. I was married to him almost ten years. My divorce from him is almost final. He turned out to be a man with many problems. I left him because I couldn't stand the violence anymore, or the other women.

The children and I now live in a town called Montague. Working at the radio station is great and I dearly love it. I've been to college for business and have two associate's degrees. Marriage to me is not a good thing, for some reason I seem to do it all wrong. We're very happy here, the school's good, the neighbors are nice and the children have lots of kids to play with.

Somehow I ended up being the neighborhood mom. It's not uncommon to find ten children here in my living room watching a movie or playing Nintendo. It's just a two-bedroom mobile home. I have a day bed in the living room which is fixed up to kinda look like the inside of a captain's quarters. The day bed is where I sleep at night. The girls share one bedroom and Scott has the other one. It sounds small but we were living in a pop-up at the campground for a month and a half, so this seems like a huge home. I kinda like it though, as we're a close-knit family.

My transportation is a full size van that seats twelve people. There are a lot of times I have all the kids in the neighborhood with me and we'll go to the beach or the sand dunes. I love having all the kids around. The neighbors think I'm crazy, but you know, Dakota, it keeps me busy, plus the kids and I are having a good time.

We also have two dogs whose names are Lassie and Beauty. I used to own a kennel where I raised collies and shelties. The children and I use to show them.

Your mom says you might not write back and that's ok too, but if you'd like to have someone to write to, I'd like to be your pen pal.

Take Care,
Dawn

Dawn finished the letter and wondered if Dakota would write back. She wouldn't blame him if he didn't, but she had to be honest with him. *"Bet he won't think of me as that sweet little girl anymore. Twice divorced with four kids. That sure will get him,"* Dawn thought to herself. She decided she would mail the letter the next morning on her way to work.

Checking her mailbox a week later Dawn was surprised to find a letter. She just stood there looking at the envelope and the return address. It was from Dakota Deer, Louisiana State Penitentiary. She was admiring his handwriting on the envelope. It was so fancy. She wasn't sure she wanted to open the letter. What if he told her not to write anymore? Pushing this thought aside Dawn walked into the trailer, sat down on her daybed and opened it up.

Dear Dawn,

I received your letter yesterday and it was really nice to hear from you. It's been a few years since we last talked. Yes, I was surprised you wrote.

You asked me if you could write. Well why not? It's not like I have lots of women to write to me. We've been friends for a long time, and even though we haven't stayed in contact over the years, I'd love to hear from you.

I can tell by your letter that you've had a rough go of it; and if you ever need a shoulder to lean on, just know I'm here for you. I may not be able to do much for you from prison, but know my thoughts and well wishes are with you.

I can tell you think the world of your children. They are really blessed for having a mom like you. Children are precious and more people ought to realize that like you do.

You know I really have to look up to you for the way you're handling your situation. Having four children and working is a lot of work. You must have a lot of patience. You seem to handle it all very well.

I'm going to let you go for now and will write to you, my friend, later. You just stay as sweet as you are, and don't work too hard. Tell everyone I said hi and be good in school.

With all my thoughts,
Dakota

As Dawn read the letter tears formed in her eyes. Dakota was still her friend. He wanted to give her moral support. She had never had that in either of her two marriages. No one had ever been there for her. She was always the one who had to be there for them. Grabbing a tissue, Dawn wiped the tears from her eyes and placed Dakota's letter in her top dresser drawer.

"Mom, are you all right? Why are you crying?" Leigh was standing by the day bed.

Dawn turned around, "No honey, Mom's not sad. These are happy tears. An old friend of mine wrote me a letter, and it was so sweet, it made me cry."

"Who wrote to you and made you cry?"

Dawn picked up her daughter, sat her on the day bed, and sat down beside her. "Well, his name is Dakota Deer. I knew him when I was a teenager. He was a really nice friend to me back then. He's Cheryl's son but lives in Louisiana now. Cheryl gave me his address. I wrote to him and asked him if he would like to be my pen pal. He answered yes. His nice letter made me so happy I cried."

"Why is he living so far away, Mom? Doesn't he miss his Mommy?" Leigh asked. Dawn thought to herself a moment, now what do I say? I guess the truth is the only way to go with this one.

"Well, he's in prison now. He did something bad when he was young and has had to stay there a long time."

"What did he do that was bad?" Leigh asked.

"He ugh... he ugh... well, he was in a fight with a bad man and killed him. The man had a gun and was trying to take some of Dakotas's things. While defending himself, Dakota killed the man." Dawn wondered what Leigh's reaction to this would be. Leigh surprised her mom.

"Well that bad man shouldn't have tried to take Dakota's things, Mom. That was wrong. I'll bet Dakota is lonely. Mom, can I write to him too?"

"Let me write to him and see what he says ok? But I'll bet

he would really like it if you would color him a picture." Bouncing off the bed, Leigh ran off to the cupboard for her crayons and coloring book. She sat up at the kitchen table and started to color a picture for Dakota.

Dawn's other three children walked into the house. "What ya doing Leigh?" Lynn asked. "I'm coloring a picture for mom's friend, he's in prison for killing a bad man. I'm coloring him a picture, to make him happy."

"Well, we want to color him a picture too," Lynn said. As all four children sat around the table coloring Dakota a picture, Dawn decided this was a good time to make supper.

"His name is Dakota and Mom knew him when she was little. They are pen pals now. Mom's going to send our pictures to him. He lives far away and can't see his mommy, so this will make him happy," Leigh said proudly to her brother and sisters.

Dawn listened to her children talk as they colored their pictures. She was so proud of them. They were so caring about other people's feelings. The fact that Dakota was in prison for murder didn't seem to bother any of them one bit. All they cared about was sending this man a little bit of happiness.

After supper the children had their pictures done and wanted to know if they could go outside and ride their bikes. Dawn asked them first to put their names and ages on their pictures so that Dakota would know whom each picture was from and how old they were. After each child did this, out the door they went. Dawn looked at the pictures. The children had colored their best. *"This will surely put a smile on his face,"* Dawn thought.

With the children outside, Dawn walked over to her day bed and sat down to write Dakota a letter. *"I sure hope he doesn't mind that I told the children where he is and why I believe in honesty, and I'm sure he'll understand."*

Dear Dakota,

The children are outside riding their bikes so I thought this would be a good time to start a letter to you. I hope you don't mind, but I told my children about you, where you are, and why. I believe in being honest with them. Enclosed you will find four pictures from them. They thought this would make you happy.

I was really pleased that you wrote me back. In fact, to tell you the truth, it made my day. I will try to write to you often. Maybe I can put a smile on your face once in a while.

Today work went great. I really love working for the radio station. I've never done anything like this before, and it's really neat. I go to clients and sell them air time. Then I get to write the commercials and produce them. I take them back to the client. If the commercial is approved, it goes on the air.

You wrote in your letter that working and having four children must be tough and that I seem to handle it well. The truth is, not always. Sometimes I get down and wish I could get more for the children then I do. That's not to say that they are lacking in food or anything like that, but sometimes I wish I could buy them the different things they want. But I guess every parent wishes that.

I do try my best with them, and we do silly things. Lou has a rock collection. Even when I'm out working if I see a rock by the side of the road that looks different I stop the van, pick it up, and bring it home to her. She keeps them in a box in her bedroom. It really makes her day.

This weekend I'm going to try to hook up my washer and dryer out on the front porch. That ought to be fun since I haven't got a clue as to what I'm doing. The front porch is enclosed, since the trailer is so small, I thought that would be a good place to put them. I'll bet you're going to laugh when I tell you how it will work! I'm going to hook up a garden hose to my washer and then to my sink. Are you laughing yet? I sure am.

This weekend I'm also going to take the kids to the dunes

and try and teach them to sand surf. Remember when we use to do that as kids? I'm sure they'll end up with lots of sand in their mouths. I'll have to take pictures.

If you ever get a chance to call, I'd love to talk with you. My phone number is at the bottom of this letter.

Your mom tells me that you are into woodworking. So what do you make? She also told me you do leather work. I think this sounds really neat. You'll have to write and tell me about it.

Guess I'll close for now, since the kid's pictures will make the letter thick. I'll write again soon.

Take Care,
Dawn

Chapter 11

As Dakota walked up to one of the agents in the surveillance team he said, "Agent Raymond. So how's it going?"

"Agent Deer we weren't expecting you. Did you get my report Sir?" Agent Raymond replied.

"Yes I did, Agent Raymond, but I just thought I'd come see for myself. You don't mind do you?" Dakota asked.

"No Sir, not at all. The children are out riding their bikes. We have agents keeping an eye on them. Ms. Brown is in the trailer sitting on her couch. She appears to be writing, Sir."

"Good. Now if you don't mind, I'd like to have a look through your binoculars." Taking the binoculars from Agent Raymond, Dakota watched Dawn. She was sitting on her day bed curled up writing. She looked so lonely. *"How I would just love to hug her and tell her everything is going to be all right,"* Dakota thought.

Bringing Dakota back from his thoughts, Agent Raymond asked, "Sir, if you don't mind my asking, why are we watching this woman and her four children?"

Dakota spun on him, "Agent Raymond, do you have any clue as to who I am or whom you're talking to?"

"Well, ah... yes sir," Agent Raymond answered wishing he had never asked.

"Then let me remind you of something. You take your assignments, do your job, report your findings, and never ask why or for how long your assignment might be for. Do you understand?"

"Yes Sir, Agent Deer."

"Good now that we understand each other let me also remind you of this. That lady and her four children are under our government's protection. It is yours and the other agent's job to see to it that not a hair on their heads is harmed in any way. Do I make myself clear?" Dakota asked.

"Yes Sir. Thank you, Sir. I will do that, Sir," Agent Raymond answered him.

"Now I have to be going, keep up the good work." And with that Dakota left.

Letting out a long breath, Agent Raymond thought to himself, *"Way to go, Raymond, piss off Agent Deer, good way to make brownie points."*

A week later Dakota had received his second and third letters from Dawn. The letters got better as they went. She was opening up to him. The pictures the children colored with every letter touched his heart. I have to call her. Walking over to the phone in the living room Dakota glanced at his watch. The children should be in bed by now. As the phone rang on the other end, Dakota got a little nervous. He could hear the operator asking Dawn if she would accept the collect call from Inmate Dakota Deer at a correctional facility. Dawn said yes. "Hey, what's new?" Dakota asked. Dawn's voice sounded like an angel's to him.

"Dakota, I'm so glad you called. I've been thinking so much about you."

"I know I can tell by the letters you write. Dawn, you can't even know how good it made me feel that you told the kids where I'm at and why. To know they still care enough to color pictures for me is really great. You are doing a great job with the kids."

"Thanks Dakota, that means a lot. So how have you been?" she asked.

"Well, I'd be better if you would send me pictures of you and the kids. It would mean a lot to me."

Dawn hesitated, "Well um, I have some great pictures of the kids I could send you."

"That's great, but I kinda would like to see Mommy too. Now you're not getting shy on me are you Dawn?"

"No, it's not that Dakota, it's just well...you know I'm not sixteen anymore and well I've had a few kids...and well...I'm not in...um as good as shape as I used to be," Dawn said shyly.

"Dawn that really doesn't matter. I'm not after your body, girl, I'm after what's inside your heart. You could be as big as the moon, or as small as a pea, and it wouldn't matter to me. It's what's on the inside of a person that counts. Being in prison has taught me that. I'm not like the men on the outside. They look at a woman and want her to be a model and forget about her feelings and what she's really all about. I'm not like that, Dawn," Dakota said.

"Ok, Dakota, you win, I'll send you a few pictures. Then you also have to send me a few of you."

"All right it's a deal. Now I also need to talk to you about something else. Dawn, you know where I'm at."

"Yes, Dakota."

"Do you understand I have a life sentence? I know that someday I'll be getting out of here Dawn, I just don't know for sure when."

"Yes Dakota, I understand that," she said a little let down. *"Here it comes,"* she thought, *"the big push off."*

"Well, I want you to understand that I'll do the best I can for you and those darling children of yours. I wish I could be there to help you, because I really do care. But Dawn, I want you to think of something and really think about it. Maybe I'm jumping the gun here, but I want you to understand that getting involved with someone in prison can be really hard and can sometimes hurt."

"Dakota, I don't think you'd ever hurt me. I've known you too long. If you were going to do that, you would have done it by now, or years ago."

"Dawn, that's not what I mean. It could be four to five years before I get out of here. Before we go any farther, I just want you to think of that. Right now we have a good friendship, but if it goes farther; and Dawn you and I both know the direction we're heading. You need to take a step back and think. Can you wait that long or maybe longer? I would never hurt you for anything in the world, but I have no control over the time frame. I've seen couples go through this before. I just don't want you to get hurt, not now, or ever by me. Do you understand?" he said.

"Yes, Dakota I do. I've already thought about it, and I'd like you to know something too. You're the only man I've ever been able to be honest with. You're the only man who has ever cared about my feelings and who I am inside. And no, Dakota I'm not giving that up. If all I can have with you is phone calls, letters, and pictures, then that's more than I've ever had with anyone else. You give me what's inside your heart. I've never had that before. Do you understand what I'm saying, Dakota?"

"Ok, Dawn, I just had to be honest with you. I'm not trying to upset you. Please don't think that. I've just never had anyone I could reveal my innermost self to. Dawn, you're the first." He then paused and thought to himself, *"And you'll be the only, someday you'll be my wife, and those kids will be my kids."*

The conversation lasted about two hours. Dawn and Dakota caught up on old times and things they had both been through. They talked about life, relationships, kids and even the weather. They were free to be themselves. They put on no fronts for each other and in the process of things a love started to develop.

"Dawn, I really hate to go, but we're racking up your phone bill. Just let me know how much it is and I'll send you the money for the call."

"I can pay my own phone bill, Dakota."

"Look, I'm the one who called and I'll pay for it. You just take care of those kids."

"Dakota Deer...!"

"Dawn, don't argue with me. I've got the money, and I'll pay for the calls. Unless little lady, you don't want me calling again. Now just be sweet and take care of those little darlings. I'll take care of the phone. And, Mom, you can let them write to me, too, if they want; and I'll write to them. They might enjoy that," he said with a sense of humor.

Laughing, Dawn said, "All right, Dakota you win. And yes they would love that. I'll talk to you later."

"Ok. Now hang up the phone, Dawn."

"Ok, good-bye, Dakota."

When Dakota didn't answer her she said, "Dakota, aren't you going to say goodbye to me?"

"Not in a million years. Goodbyes to me, Dawn, are forever. I'll never say that to you. Now just be sweet and hang up the phone."

"Dakota, do you know how hard that is, hanging up the phone on you like that?"

"It's ok Darling, just hang it up. I'll call again, and it won't be that long before I do. When you need me, I'll be there for you. Even if it's just for a few minutes to let you know I care. You get your sleep. I know you have to be at work early in the morning. Just know I'm thinking about you. Good night darling," he said with such tenderness.

"Good night, Dakota." And with that said she hung up the phone. Then she quickly picked it back up but he was gone. The dial tone was buzzing in her ear. "I love you Dakota," she said as she placed it back in the cradle.

Dakota thought to himself, "She has no idea of the hurt this can cause her or of the loneliness it will bring her. But I'll do my best to get her through this. Somehow I'll let that woman know of the love I can give her and the children, love for a lifetime."

Walking down to his wood shop, Dakota was thinking of things he could make and send to Dawn and her children. He knew that the children like cartoons. Lynn liked Minnie Mouse, Leigh like Goofy, Lou liked Mickey Mouse, and Scott liked Donald Duck, but he had no idea what to make for Dawn.

He would work on something for the children first. "I'll make them each something cute and special. As he pulled out a few cypress knees that he had dried out, Dakota started to sand the surface of each. With that done, he began drawing Minnie Mouse on the first piece, next came the wood burning. As he began the wood burning on Minnie Mouse, Dakota's mind drifted to Dawn and the picture of her sitting on her couch. His heart ached to be there for her. If only he could be with her every day to share her daily life, and make her feel safe during the night.

As the hours passed, every detail of the characters came to life. Dakota knew he should head for bed, but the children weighed heavy on his mind. I could be a good dad for them. Teach them what life has to offer. Take them all camping, fishing, take Scott hunting, heck I might even find a hunter or two in the girls.

He knew he was hooked. In the end, his heart could also be hurt. *"But someday, somehow, someway, I'll be home with them. Then we'll all be happy. I only hope Dawn can wait that long for me. I'll show her what real love from the heart is all about. Something she's never had before nor will again with anyone else. To have her and those darling children will make my life complete."* With these thoughts heavy on his mind Dakota put the wood- working away and headed up to the house. I need to write her and let her know these things.

My Dearest Dawn,
You've been on my mind tonight and even though we've only been off the phone for a few hours, I'm missing you already!

I know we talked a lot about the future and what it may hold for each of us. I believe that someday we will be together and I'll be home with you and the children. How I look forward to that day.

I told you that for me to share myself with a woman is something I take very seriously. To open up my deepest thoughts to someone isn't something I've ever done.

I can't thank you enough for writing to me, for now look at what we have started. Maybe the Lord in all His wisdom saved me for a woman like you.

You say that I make your day with my letters. Honey, you make my day with the letters you write to me. The perfume you spray on your letters drives me crazy. Make sure you never run out of that.

You kept asking me on the phone about me loving a woman with four children and did I know what I was getting into. I know this must bother you, but Darling, a woman like you doesn't come along every day. I can see that you truly care for your children.

Honey, that only makes you more special to me. You put your children first and I admire you for that. But you're having four children doesn't bother me. It just gives me a family to love and share with.

Now stop your worrying and know that Dakota will be here for you. Am I moving to fast for you? If so let me know, but it's so hard when I have someone so wonderful like you in my life.

I've been working with a new puppy lately. His name is Bear. He's a Catahoula Cure. That's the leopard dog for the state of Louisiana. I hope to train him to be a drug and tracking dog.

I've told you about working with the state troopers and their dogs. I really enjoy that. We have drug, attack, tracking, bomb and other working dogs. As you can tell, I stay pretty busy, but never too busy to have time for you.

I will call you again this weekend. Until then know my thoughts are with you and the children. You be good and I will be too.

Love,
Dakota

Finishing the letter, Dakota sat and thought about Dawn and the children. Would she understand and believe he meant everything he said to her. Dawn had been through two bad marriages and the men in her past had treated her badly. Somehow he wanted to show her that not all men were like that. Dakota knew he was different and when he loved it was for life. *"Somehow I'll show her more love than she's ever known,"* he thought, *"but first I have to finish my time and then someday I'll make it right for her and the children."*

As the months flew by, Dawn and Dakota were grew closer every day. The letters arrived at the prison daily for Dakota and the happiness he felt was beyond his wildest dreams. Dawn felt this same happiness as she went to her mailbox. The letters from Dakota were breathtaking. Dakota was even writing to the children. Not every day like he did Dawn, but once a week each child could look forward to a letter from Dakota.

It was Dawn's daughter, Leigh, who wrote to Dakota the most. The other children looked forward to his phone calls. Leigh would write to Dakota at least twice a week. She would ask him all kinds of questions tell him about her boyfriend. She even told him how they had learned to sand surf on the sand dunes. Dakota enjoyed the children very much. To him they were his family.

One day while having coffee with her friend, Cindy, Dawn was talking about Dakota.

"He's such a part of me, Cindy, I couldn't even think about life without Dakota in it. I love him so much. His phone calls and letters mean the world to me. I have the love of a life time."

"Do you understand how crazy this sounds Dawn? You're in love with a man in prison, for murder no less, and serving a life sentence to boot. How can you love someone you haven't spent any time with? People just don't fall in love through letters and over the phone."

"But Dakota's going to get out someday, and then we'll be together. Oh Cindy he makes me so happy. I've never felt so loved."

"Dawn, wake up and smell the coffee! Dakota can't be here

with you, he can't hold you, kiss you, he can't be a father figure to your children. There are men out there who would love to date you. You keep turning them down and for what? Some guy who's in prison, who can never be there for you? I'm not saying Dakota's all bad, but he's not here, and well Dawn you've got to get on with your life. Look, I know Dakota thinks that someday he'll be out of prison, but lets get real Dawn. The man has a life sentence. Do you hear me a LIFE SENTENCE? Every con says they'll be getting out, but Honey, cons with a life sentence just don't get out. That's why they call it life!" Cindy said.

"I can't explain it, Cindy, but I believe him. I can't walk away from the best thing that's ever happened to me."

"Ok now let me ask you something. Please understand I'm only asking because I care. Are you sure you're not in love with Dakota, just because he's safe?"

"I don't think I understand what you mean by safe?"

"Well for example, he can't beat you, he can't cheat on you, and he can't drink too much, or use drugs. He can't be the demanding husband who wants you to pick up his dirty socks, or have supper on the table right when he walks in. He can't force you to have sex with him anytime he wants, even if you're not up to it. Dawn, are you sure that your heart is really in love with him and not your head?"

Dawn couldn't believe what her friend was saying. She was a grown woman; of course she knew what her heart felt. Dakota's letters made her days and when he called that made her evenings. The thought of not having Dakota in her life brought her close to tears. "Of course I know what I feel Cindy. It's more love than I've ever felt in my life. Dakota's my soul mate."

"Well just don't go locking yourself up with him. Life is too short, Dawn. Just remember he's the one in prison not you! You have your whole life a head of you. Don't let it pass you by."

"Cindy, I would marry the man in prison if he'd only ask me. Does that tell you how much I love him? If all I can have the rest of my life with Dakota is his letters and phone calls and the love he shows me through them, then I would have more than most people out here who have their husbands every night."

This stunned Cindy. She had never seen Dawn so sure of herself before and she had known Dawn since they were children. What could she say to that? "As long as you're happy, then that's all that matters."

"I am Cindy, more than I've ever been. If the Lord were to take me tomorrow, I would have at long last known what it felt like to be loved and what he does for my children. He's been more of a father to them then they've ever had in their life. They love him as much as I do."

"I must admit Dawn, I have seen a change in the children. They seem to be more content then I've ever seen them. They aren't withdrawn like they used to be. At first I thought it was just because of your being divorced. But I've got to admit when the children do talk about Dakota they really do light up," Cindy said.

Later that evening the children were all in their pajamas. The movie they had been watching with Dawn was just rolling through the credits, when the phone rang. Leigh got up and said, "I'll get it." She walked over to the phone and said hello. Dawn looked over at Leigh. Her daughter wasn't saying anything, but the smile Leigh had on her face told Dawn that it was Dakota. Dakota would take his turn talking to each of the children, and wish them a good night, before he would talk to Dawn.

"Good evening, and how is my little lady tonight? I just thought I'd call and check on you kids and make sure that Mom was being nice to you. She is, isn't she?" Dakota asked.

Leigh just laughed. "Yes Dakota, Mom's being nice. We just got done watching a video. It was really a good movie. It's called, *The Little Mermaid.*"

"Oh really, and was she a good mermaid? Was she afraid of the sharks?" he teased.

"Well the witch had a few sharks in the movie, but they didn't hurt the little mermaid. Hey Dakota, did you get my letter? You know the one with my picture in it?"

"Yes I did. I got all your school pictures, but I was just wondering something, Leigh. Since they took your pictures sitting on a paint ladder and you were holding a paint bucket and brush in your hand, does that mean you can help me paint in my wood shop when I get home?" Dakota asked.

"Sure if you want us to. I guess the school must know that we have talent," Leigh said proudly.

"All right it's a deal, I'll put you kids to work with me in my wood shop when I get home. Maybe we'll even let your mom help. Do you think she has any talent?"

"I doubt it, Mom can't even draw a stick man. Maybe you'd better let her do the sanding."

Dakota couldn't help but laugh at this. Children were the sweetest things and they were honest. "I'll take your word for it. The sand master is who she'll be. Now speaking of sand, don't you think it's time for the sand man? After all, I've got the other kids to talk to yet and I don't want to get into trouble with your mom for keeping you up past your bed time."

"Ok Dakota, I'll talk to you later, Good night."

"You be good Leigh and help your mom around the house, sweet dreams, little lady."

Dakota took his turn talking with the other children. He had them laughing. He enjoyed these children. As they each said good night to him, Dakota would listen, as Dawn would tuck each one in bed and kiss them good night. *"Someday I'll be there to say good night to them too,"* he thought.

Now it was his and Dawn's turn to talk. "So Darling, now that the children are all tucked in it's just you and me."

"Dakota, you just make their day when you call like that.

75

They love talking to you."

"I like putting a smile on their faces, Dawn. Your children are special. You know I love them as if they were my own. Children need to know that they are loved and that they have someone they can talk to or lean on if they need them. I try to give that to them. It's not easy to for me being here with you all there, but I try to find ways the best I can to close that gap. So tell me how is Mommy today?"

"I'm fine," Dawn said.

"That's it, you're fine? I can tell by your voice something's bothering you. Want to talk about it?" Dakota asked.

"Well, today I was over to my girlfriend's house, you know Cindy. I've talked to you about her before. Anyway we were talking about you, the kids and me. She just doesn't understand how I can feel about you the way I do. She seems to think I should date."

"And how do you feel about it?" He knew people would give Dawn a hard time about loving a man in prison, but he knew she could handle it.

"What do you mean? You know how I feel about you. I don't want to date anyone, I'm in love with you, and I'll wait however long it takes. Dakota, I've never had anyone give me the amount of love and respect that you do. What are you saying, that you want me to date?" Dawn was getting a little upset now, but he knew if he got her to vent a little she would feel better.

"No, that's not what I said, but maybe your girlfriend is right. Maybe you should get out a little. Dawn, I don't expect you to just sit home all the time. I've told you that before. Maybe you should go out to a movie, go to dinner, go dancing. Don't just sit home, it makes the waiting longer." *"Here it comes now,"* he thought *"she'll blow on this one, but she needs to let it all out."*

And as expected, she did blow. "Dakota Deer, what has gotten into you? Dancing, Oh that's a fine idea! But there's just one problem, the only place to dance is in a bar. I see, so now you want to send me to the meat market. When other men want to dance with me and put their hands all over me, that won't bother you a bit. What a grand idea! Let's see next you're going to tell me to go have sex with other men," Dawn said sharply.

He quickly thought to himself, "*Maybe the dancing wasn't a good thing to bring up, I should have just suggested a movie and dinner. Now you have a hot little filly on your hands Dakota, quick think of something to calm her down.*" Tenderly and with much love Dakota replied.

"Darling, all I'm saying is, I completely trust you with my heart. I know you'd never do anything to hurt me. I trust the fact that you could go anywhere anytime and I know my love is safe with you. Our love is something we both cherish and hold dear. We don't take it lightly and because of this we have a wonderful trust and faith in each other. I'm not one to say you can't do this or that. I want you to do things and wherever you go, just know, my love is always with you."

The other end of the phone was quiet, but Dakota knew Dawn was still there. He hadn't meant to make her cry, but he knew he had touched her deeply. Dakota and Dawn had talked about their love many times but up to this point, they had never said the three words most lovers say.

"Dawn, you know something? I really do love you. Maybe I should have told you sooner, but Darling, I would rather show you my love, not just talk about it," Dakota said.

Dawn tried to speak, but a lump was stuck in her throat. She cleared her voice and said, "Dakota, you know I love you, more than anything in the world. I just couldn't stand it if I didn't have you and your love in my life. I wish you were here. I need you, Dakota."

His heart was being ripped apart, knowing Dawn needed him to put his arms around her, to comfort her, to let her know she was safe and loved. He knew he shouldn't say this to her, but he had to. In the end it would hurt her more, but they both needed it.

"Darling, why don't you and the children come and see me. I'll send you the money and I'll arrange for a special visit. It'll take a month or so to get all the paperwork done, but I think we need to see each other."

The tears stopped and the excitement was back in her voice. "Dakota, what are you talking about? A special visit?"

"The visiting hours are from nine to four on Saturdays and Sunday. An inmate can have a visitor twice a month, but for only a couple of hours each visit. I don't want our visit to be behind the glass, so let me make the arrangements so we can visit down at the main camp. I'll have the prison send you the paperwork."

"Paperwork, I don't understand Dakota?"

"I first need to get you on my visiting list. The prison will send you paperwork. Fill it out and then send it back to the prison, and then once it's processed they'll send you an approval letter. When you come to visit me, you'll have to have this letter with you. Don't worry Honey, things will be just fine and we'll have a nice visit," Dakota said.

"Oh Dakota, we're really going to see each other? The children have two weeks off for spring break. Maybe that would be a good time to come for a visit. That's in a month and a half." She was bubbling with excitement.

"Perfect, that will work out just fine. The weather will be nice down here then, not too hot or muggy, and the trip will do you and the children a lot of good. Now Dawn, you need to get the directions from my mom on how to get here. She and Rich come down twice a year and go different ways each time. She'll tell you which way is the best to travel. I don't want you to rush down. You all stop and stay somewhere; I don't want my darling driving when she's tired. When you get here, there's a nice hotel called the Saint Francis Ville Inn. It's about five miles away from the prison. Mom and Rich stay there and just love it. It's real southern style and my mom says the pool is unique. When we know the dates you're coming call ahead and make reservations there."

"I will Dakota! The children and I are going out to your mom's this weekend. I'll get the directions then. I can't wait to tell the kids in the morning. They'll be so excited. We haven't been on a trip since we went to Kentucky last year to see my friend Nancy and her children. You remember me talking about her to you?"

"Yes, I do. Maybe you should stop there and visit her for a night or two before coming down here, give yourself and the children a break from the road. Where was it in Kentucky you said she lived?"

"Providence, only about forty-five minutes from Fort Campbell," Dawn said.

"Hang on, let me get my road atlas out and have a look see a minute, I'll be right back," Dakota said.

While waiting for Dakota to get the road atlas Dawn walked over to the coffee pot to pour herself a cup of coffee. In her excitement Dawn missed the cup and poured coffee all over the counter. She laughed at herself, as she cleaned it up. "Dawn, you're acting like a school girl going out on her first date," she said to herself.

"What are you talking about?" Dakota said.

Dawn hadn't realized that Dakota was back to the phone already. "Oh nothing, I was just talking to myself. While you were gone, I poured myself a cup of coffee, I was so excited I missed the cup and got coffee all over the counter."

"You didn't get burned, did you?"

Feeling a little embarrassed Dawn answered him, "No, not at all, just made a mess."

"Honey, you have to be more careful. Now look, I've got the atlas out to see how far Providence is from here. It looks to me to be about ten or eleven hours."

"That's great, it takes me about ten hours to get to Nancy's from here. That would mean she's about halfway there. That would be perfect," Dawn said with excitement.

"Maybe you should call your friend Nancy. She and the kids might enjoy riding down to Louisiana with you. They could stay at the hotel and enjoy the pool, while your visiting me. The town of Saint Francis Ville has a lot of neat shops. There are plantations to see also. You could make a really nice trip out of it for you all to enjoy."

"Dakota, the only thing I really want to see on this trip is the man I love. The one I miss with all my heart."

"Honey, I know that. It's just that I want to make this trip really mean something to you and the children. Something you can really enjoy. For when my darlings are happy, so am I. Well Sweetheart, I'd better let you go, so you can get your rest."

"I'm not tired Dakota, really I'm not," Dawn said with a yawn.

"Dawn, I can hear it in your voice. Now just be sweet and go get ready for bed. I'll call you tomorrow. Give those darling kids a hug for me in the morning and tell them I'm thinking of them too."

"All right you win, it was a long day. Good night Dakota, I love you and thank you."

"No Darling, it's I who should be thanking you. You have given me five people to love and cherish and all you get is one. Seems to me that I'm coming out ahead. Good night, my Darling, I will see you in my dreams."

"And I shall see you too. Good night." With that Dawn slowly hung up the phone. This time she didn't pick up the phone to see if he was still there. No, it was better just to leave it alone and just tell herself he would always be in reach.

Dakota sat and looked at the phone. His heart ached. He wanted to be there with her right now and hold her. Hell, what he really wanted was to marry the woman, be in her bed every night, and to wake up every morning with all the commotion four children can make getting ready for school. He knew he had a family back in Michigan waiting on him. The thought made him smile. "Mr. and Mrs. Dakota Deer and family." He liked the sounds of that. He wondered what Dawn and the children would think of it. Maybe I should just make it happen and see what my darling would think of that. A nice letter tonight is in order for Mrs. Deer.

Dear Mrs. Deer,
The first thing on my mind is that I love you and oh so much. I guess by the opening of this letter you can see what the other thing is. I've been thinking a lot about us just so you know; I do feel like you're my wife. I wonder now, is that ok with you? Just joking, Honey. I already know it is. As you've seen by now I also addressed the envelope to Mrs. Dakota Deer. I'll bet that made you smile. I know I was when I wrote it.

Enclosed you will find the money for the phone bill. I know what you're saying, but Honey, I told you that I would take care of it. I'm not a lazy man and I can pay for it. So you just quit your fretting and let me have my way on this. Ok? Good, now that's settled we can move onto other things.

I want to make you a ring. That way everyone will know that you're a woman who has a husband. It will make me feel good to know you're wearing my ring. I want you to go and get your finger sized for a wide band. I have something special in mind for you. I know how you like silver. The ring I'll make for you will be made out of European silver. They have the purest silver around. No sterling for my wife. When I make something, Honey, I do it the right way or not at all.

I'm looking forward to our visit. I can't tell you how much it will mean to me to see you and the children. Someday we won't have to visit, we'll be together.

You will find that I am a very serious man when it comes to our family. Family means the world to me. To know that I have a wife like you and four darling children makes my day.

Well Mrs. Deer, this will be a short letter. As you can see I've sent along a few more pictures of me.

You get your sleep and know that Dakota is always close by. I will always make sure you and the children are safe until I can be there with you.

With all my love,
Your husband,
Dakota

Chapter 12

The very next week Dawn received the paper work from the prison. She filled it out and sent it back the same day. Now if the prison approved her for Dakota's visiting list, she would be one more step closer to seeing the man she loved. Or as Dakota would say, she would be on her way to seeing her husband.

Dawn talked to Nancy about the trip to the prison. Nancy thought it was a great idea. She said that Dakota was right and that Dawn and the children should stay a few days with her in Kentucky before going on to Louisiana to see Dakota. Nancy had known Dawn for years and knew that this man must be special for Dawn to make a trip to a prison.

Dawn's family, to her surprise, was very supportive of her going to see Dakota. Her brothers and sisters didn't see the harm in it. They thought that maybe once she saw Dakota she would realize that loving a man in prison was a waste of time.

Her father on the other hand, had seen the change in Dawn and knew that she was deeply in love. He had also seen the children and their contentment. From the way they talked about Dakota it was obvious they loved him.

A few nights later, Dawn's brother in Georgia called her. He was in the army and just got back from Germany six months earlier. He called to tell her that he was being shipped over to Desert Storm. He had been in the service for years and was due to retire in six months. "Dawn," he said, "I've been in Vietnam and all over for my country, but this time I have a feeling if I go, I'll come back in a body bag." Dawn could tell he was really scared. Dawn was close to her brother, Mike, and tried to encourage him.

The phone call was still bothering her when Dakota called later that night. "Hey honey, what's up with my little family in Michigan?"

"Oh Dakota it's just rotten. The Army is sending my brother over to Desert Storm and he's due to retire in six months. He's been in Vietnam already and I'm sure if they send him, he won't come back alive. Dakota, I'm really scared."

"Where is he stationed, Honey? What's his rank, and full name?" Dawn had no idea why Dakota was asking all these questions, but she answered him.

"Don't worry, Honey. Your brother won't be going," Dakota reassured her.

"Dakota, you can't know that. They say that he's leaving in twenty-four hours."

"Trust me, I have a way of knowing these things. Just have faith."

"But Dakota, how do you know and how can you be so sure?" Dawn asked.

"Let me tell you something, Honey. I just know. Now tell me about those darling children of yours. How are their grades in school and are they helping mom around the house?"

"Oh Dakota, they're grades in school are great, and as far as helping around the house. Why I can't begin to tell you what a difference your talking to them makes. What would I ever do without you?" Dawn said, pleased.

"Well, little lady, you will never find out. Like I've told you before, I take things in my life very seriously. You and those children are my life and now I have a reason to get out of here. It will be hard on us for a while being apart, but once we're together you will see the happiness we shall all have. And, Dawn, it's going to be a happiness you've never had before. You will always know if something gets on your nerves that I will be there to take care of it."

"Dakota, you have no idea how I depend on you now. If it wasn't for your love, I know I'd truly be lost."

"Well I found you, just like the cypress knee I made you says, I was very lucky to find you, and you know the Leprechaun never lies," Dakota teased her.

Dawn was thinking back to the day when she received the package from Dakota. In it was a cypress knee, with a wood burning on it of a Leprechaun holding a pot of gold. Above his head were the words, "I was very lucky to find you." The artwork was wonderful and Dakota had told her the pot was full of Dawn's love.

Dakota had a way of expressing his love which really touched Dawn's heart. He wasn't like other men who sent cards or flowers, but he showed his love for her through his artwork. When Dakota made things for Dawn, it was with his whole heart, all the love he could put into it.

Dakota brought Dawn back out from her daydream, "Earth to Dawn. Hello Dawn this is earth. Where did you go, Dawn?"

"I'm here. I was just daydreaming about the day I received the Leprechaun you made me. Isn't it funny to think that years ago we were just friends? Now look at us."

"The Lord has a way of making things turn out for the best. With faith in Him anything is possible. Now let me let you go, Darling, as I've got some work to do tonight. You just be sweet for me and give those children my love."

"I will Dakota, just remember that my love is with you now and always."

" I love you, Dawn."

"I love you, Dakota. Good night."

"Good night. I'll talk to you later." And then he was gone.

It didn't seem to matter how much Dawn talked to Dakota or how many letters she received from him, she missed him terribly, but she thought she put up a good front for him.

Chapter 13

After Dakota made a few phone calls, Dawn's brother, Mike, was told he would not be going to Desert Storm. The rest of Mike's company went, but he was left behind. Mike found this strange, but was too relieved to question it.

A couple weeks later Dawn received a call from her brother again. He was leaving Georgia for Desert Storm. The plane was due to leave in three days. "Mike, I just don't understand it. Why do they want to send you when you're so close to retirement?" Dawn asked.

"I don't know Dawn, I guess it's just the Army. They can do whatever they want to," Mike said sounding upset.

"Dakota told me that you wouldn't be going, and just like that you didn't go. Mike, I really think the man's got a connection with God. I know it sounds crazy, but he was really sure you wouldn't go."

"Well at this point Dawn, I'll believe anything. If you talk to Dakota again, I sure wish you'd tell him to hook up with that connection with God, and ask him to keep me from going. I've spent 25 years with the service and I'd really rather not stay in any longer. If I go over to Desert Storm, I'll have to stay in another year and not by choice either," Mike told her.

"It's Friday night and Dakota always calls on Friday night. It can't hurt to ask."

"And Sis, it wouldn't hurt to say a few prayers either."

When Dakota called Dawn on Friday night, she told Dakota what was going on again with her brother Mike. Once again, Dakota told Dawn not to worry about it and that he'd take care of it.

Once again Dakota made a phone call to the base and had Sargent Mike Star's assignment to Desert Storm canceled. Once again Mike was transferred to another company and taken off the list to go over to Desert Storm.

When Sargent Mike Star received word that his assignment had been changed, he knew he just had to call and talk to Dawn.

"Hello," Dawn said as she answered the phone.

"Ok Sis, I believe you. You're right Dakota's got to have a connection with God. You'll never believe it. I was transferred to another company again. And no, I'm not going to Desert Storm. I just got the news an hour ago. Sis, I know before I thought you were just a little crazy for being involved with a man in prison for murder, but if the man has a connection with God like this he can't be all bad or God wouldn't be listening," Mike said soundly excited.

"I know, isn't he special, Mike? I plan on marrying that man whenever he gets out of prison. I really love him, Mike. Just wait till the day comes when you can meet him."

Mike and Dawn talked for another hour longer. They talked about Dakota mostly. Dawn felt good that at least one of her family members was at last realizing she wasn't crazy for loving Dakota the way she did.

A month went by and Dawn received the papers from the prison saying she was now on Dakota's visitors list. The letter explained all the visiting rules, the hours, and days when an inmate could have visitors. She was instructed to bring the letter the first time she came to the prison to visit. Dawn could hardly wait. The time was drawing near. At long last she would be seeing Dakota. The children were excited about the trip also. As Leigh would put it, "We're going to see our Daddy Dakota."

That evening, Dawn tucked the children in bed and then she sat on the daybed to re-read some of Dakota's letters. They warmed her heart. Dakota had told Dawn that he wouldn't be calling for a couple of days as he was going to be training state troopers and their dogs. This training would take between four and five days. He told her not to worry and that his love and thoughts would be with her.

It was late, the sun had set, and the stars were out. The moon was only at a quarter, so the night was good and dark. *"A good night for a little undercover work, well kinda anyway,"* Dakota thought to himself.

As Dakota watched Dawn through her trailer windows he could see she was growing tired. "Come on Honey, put the letters up and go to bed. You need your sleep."

Dawn stretched and put the last letter away in the cedar chest that Dakota had made for her. She turned back the daybed, and then walked to the bathroom to turn on the nightlight for the children. As she walked back through the trailer she tuned off each light as she went and then climbed into bed.

After a couple of hours of listening to the quiet of the house through his ear set, Dakota thought that the transmitters in Dawn's home surely were going to pay off tonight. He watched and when he saw no movement. He radioed to the other agents. "This is Agent Deer. I'm going in and under NO and I repeat NO conditions are any of you to make a move. I want NO radio contact until I come out. If someone in the home discovers me I will get out."

"Roger that," the other agents answered. When Dakota was satisfied that there would be radio silence, he made his move.

Quiet as a mouse, Dakota unlocked the back door. He walked down the hall and he could see Dawn was fast asleep on the daybed in the living room. As he walked over to where she slept, he softly whispered. "I'll be back Sweetheart, I just want to check on our little darlings." When he lightly walked into the girl's room, he stood there and just smiled. They were sleeping soundly and looked like little angels to him. Lou was sleeping on the bottom bunk snuggled up with her doll. Leigh and Lynn were on the top bunk with Lynn having Leigh pinned against the wall. "I'll be home soon girls," he whispered and then walked softly towards Scott's room. Scott also had a set of bunk beds in his room and Dakota found Scott sound asleep on his top bunk. Scott's bottom bunk was full of toy cars and his walls had posters of football and basketball players. "Someday soon Scott, I'll be home and then maybe we can go to a few games, and even try some hunting if you'd like," Dakota whispered to him.

Once back out in the living room Dakota stood close to Dawn as she slept. She was uncovered. Knowing he shouldn't take the risk, but unable to help himself, Dakota reached out and slowly pulled the covers over her shoulders. Dawn moved a little and slightly opened her eyes and looked right at him. Dakota froze. When she closed her eyes again, and by her breathing Dakota knew she was still asleep. "I love you Dawn," he whispered.

"I love you, Dakota," she said softly and then smiled. Dakota knew she was sleeping and would think in the morning of the pleasant dream she had last night about the two of them. He really wanted to hold her. But fought back the urge. He knew this would have to be enough until that day came.

As Dakota looked around the living room, he could see that Dawn had the things he had made her and the children everywhere. *"This is home,"* he thought, *"here with her and the children. It won't be long Darling and I'll be home."* He looked at Dawn again and his heart filled with love for her. He knew he'd better go. Being here was too much of a risk. Blowing her a kiss, he turned and left, locking the door behind him.

When Dawn woke up in the morning, she remembered dreaming of Dakota. He had been standing there next to her. It had seemed so real, especially the way he had told her that he loved her. She could only hope that someday they would be together and that all their dreams would come true.

The weeks flew by and spring break was almost here. Dawn and the children were excited about their upcoming trip to see Dakota.

"Mom, how long will it take to get to Louisiana?" Leigh asked.

"Well Leigh, I'm guessing about twenty-four hours, but we won't be in the van that long all at once. We're going to stop at Nancy's in Kentucky first and stay with her for a few days. Then Nancy and the kids will be going with us. It will then take us another eleven hours before we'll be down to where Dakota lives," Dawn answered.

"Oh Mom, I can't wait to see him. Do you think we will be able to bring Daddy Dakota home with us?" Leigh asked.

"No, I don't think he'll be able to come home with us, but Leigh I sure wish he could. Someday he'll be free. Then he'll come home to us, I'm sure of that," Dawn said.

"Mom, don't they realize that we need him up here with us, more than they need him down there? He's not a bad man and I don't think it's fair."

"I know, but Leigh, we just have to be patient. Someday when the Lord sees fit, then Dakota will be home with us."

Dawn only wished she could make Leigh understand, she knew it was hard on the children wanting him home so much. And Dawn wanted the same thing.

Sometimes, Dawn wondered if they were all fooling themselves. Would Dakota ever be a free man? She would never admit it to Dakota, but he was right, loving a man that was locked up hurt. To know the kind of love that they shared, and not be able to show each other just didn't seem fair.

A few days before Dawn and the children were to leave on their trip, Dawn's brother Mike called.

"Well Sis, it looks like three strikes and I'm out. I've got orders to go to Desert Storm and they say there's no way out of it this time," Mike said.

"Oh Mike, this just can't be. You're due to get out in just two months. How can they send you now?"

"It's the Army sis, and they can do anything they want. I don't understand it either. I've spent all these years in the service and now that I'm due to retire this comes up. I don't mind saying that JoHana and the kids are worried too."

"Can't you request an early out?"

"Not now, it's a little late for that. It would take a miracle to keep me from going this time. I should only be gone for six months. They can't extend my contract for longer than that unless the U.S. is in a direct war," he said sounding defeated.

Dawn was really upset by this news. "Mike, if Dakota calls I'll tell him what's going on. I know he should be calling before the kids and I leave for Louisiana. I know it sounds crazy but he was right the two other times, and you didn't go."

"You can tell him Sis, but I really don't think it will help this time. I love you Dawn. Tell the kids I love them too. I've got to go. I want to spend time with Jo and the kids. We've got things to get settled before I go."

"I love you Mike. Tell Jo and the kids I'll be thinking about them and you too. Don't give up faith yet. I just feel something good's going to happen," Dawn said trying to sound encouraging.

"Well if it does, you'll be the first person I let know. Talk to you later. Bye," Mike said.

"I'll be waiting for that call. Bye."

The next evening the phone rang and Lynn answered the phone, it was Dakota.

"Hey, and how is one of my favorite women in the world?" Dakota asked her.

"Just fine Dakota," Lynn said.

"How's school going? Your mom sent me your report card and you had all A's and B's, I'm really proud of you."

"Thanks Dakota. School is great. I meet a really nice boy in my class and I think he likes me," Lynn said happily.

"Oh yea, and do you like him?"

Lynn laughed. "Yes he's very cute. He carries my books to class for me."

"That sounds like a really nice gentleman. Just you be sure

he doesn't try kissing you," Dakota said with a smile.

"Oh, Dakota!" Lynn said with embarrassment.

"Hey is your mom around?"

"She's outside right now. Let me go get her." Laying the phone down, Lynn rushed outside to tell Dawn that Dakota was on the phone.

Out of breath from running into the house Dawn answered the phone, "H-e-l-l-o."

"You all right? You didn't have to run Honey, I wasn't going to hang up or anything."

"Just talk to me, Dakota, while I catch my breath. I was outside playing basketball with the kids. I didn't even hear the phone."

"So was the old folks winning or did the youngsters beat ya'll?" Dakota couldn't help but laugh.

"We were playing horse, and I was holding my own," she said still somewhat out of breath.

"So that's what you call it, when the kids are beating the tar out of you," he teased her.

"Something like that, it just sounds better."

"I talked to Lynn for a few minutes before I had her go out and get you. Seems she likes this really cute boy in school. She says he carries her books to class for her."

"Isn't it sweet Dakota? She told me that they even held hands once during a school play."

"Won't be long Mom, and they'll be growing up on us. Time sure does fly."

"I know, it doesn't seem that long ago that they were all wearing diapers."

"I called to talk to you about your trip down here. Did you get the money all right?" he asked.

"Yes Dakota, I did. Don't you think you went a little overboard with the amount you sent?"

"No, I don't. I wanted to make sure you and the children have enough. You might find something that you want on the way down here."

"The only thing I want, Dakota, is to be in your arms," she said wishfully.

"I know Honey, and that day will come, you just keep hanging on to that thought. So how is everyone doing up there?"

"You'll never believe it, Dakota, but Mike's being sent to Desert Storm. They are extending his enlistment by six months. I didn't think they could do that so close to retirement. He only has two months left and he retires." Dawn sounded upset.

"When did you hear this?" Dakota asked.

"Mike called yesterday and told me. What do you think Dakota? Can they really do this?"

"Yea Honey, the Army can do whatever they want, but don't worry about it, he's not going to go this time either. I just have a good feeling about it," Dakota said.

"Are you sure Dakota, what if all the prayers don't work this time?"

"I wasn't wrong before was I?" Dakota said.

"Dakota, I just don't understand how do you know these things?"

"Don't worry about it, Honey, I just have my ways."

"Dakota you make it sound like you have a straight line to God."

"Just trust me, Honey. Your brother will be home safe and sound. You did say he was moving to Michigan when he gets out didn't you?"

"Yes that's what they want to do. They have their house up for sale in Georgia. They want to move back home to be closer to the family."

"Guess that means I'll be getting to meet him when I come home."

"I don't know Dakota, it just all depends. Maybe you'll be tired of me by then," Dawn said with a smile that Dakota could hear in her voice.

"You think so? Do you think I should trade you in for a younger model? Maybe I should start looking now. I'm just teasing you, Honey. I could never grow tired of your love or the sweetness you show. Now, on your way down here, you just be careful and take care of those children for me."

"I will Dakota, I can't wait to get there."

"No speeding. Ya hear me? When you get here to the prison, make sure you give them that letter they sent you."

"I already have it packed. The kids and I are ready to leave. We're leaving Sunday morning. We'll be in Kentucky by Sunday evening at Nancy's," Dawn said with the excitement a child would have.

"I'll call you again Saturday night then. I've got to let you go. Give the kids a hug and kiss for me. I love you, Dawn."

"I love you, Dakota."

After Dakota broke off the call to Dawn, Dakota then picked up the phone again and dialed direct to the President's private line. "Hello, this is the President."

"Mr. President, this is Agent Deer."

"Agent Deer, it's good to hear from you. How have you been?"

"Fine, thank you, Mr. President. I need your help."

"Agent Deer your country is indebted to you in more ways than one. How can I be of service to you?" asked the President.

"I need to ask a personal favor, Mr. President."

"Name it Agent Deer. Tell me what I can do for you."

"I need a Sargent Mike Starr who is stationed in Georgia, who's due to retire in two months, to be pulled from the Desert Storm roster. The Sargent has been pulled from the list twice now. I have talked to the base Brigadier General twice, but now the Sargent has been put back on the roster once again. I feel that Sargent Starr needs to be given an early retirement and not sent to Desert Storm. Sargent Starr has been in Vietnam more than once and has received more than one Medal of Honor. He has served his country well. To extend his service at this time would be in poor taste by our military."

"I agree. I will take care of this right away. Sargent Starr will receive his retirement in just a few days. You can be sure I will have quite a chat with the Brigadier General. You say you called and talked to him twice? And this is happening again? Well, I should be thanking you, Agent Deer, for making me aware of this."

"Thank you, Mr. President."

"Thank you for calling, Agent Deer, and if I can ever be of service to you, please call again. Take care, Agent Deer."

"Good night and thank you, Mr. President," Dakota said as he hung up the phone.

A weight was taken off Dakota's mind. The President would take care of it, and Dakota was glad that he wasn't in the brigadier general's shoes. The President respected the men and women of the military. When someone was this close to retirement something like this should not be happening. Dakota also knew that the President respected him. The brigadier general would find out that if Agent Deer requested something it should be done.

Dawn's brother would be safe now and Dawn wouldn't have to worry anymore about his safety.

The next day Dawn was visiting her friend Cindy. Cindy had agreed to keep an eye on things for Dawn while she and the children were gone on their trip.

"I can't thank you enough for watching the house while we're gone. I've had the mail stopped. Since the dogs are over here at your house there's really not much for you to do. Maybe just go over every few days and check things out. My plants should be all right until I get back."

"Are you sure you and the kids will be all right alone on this trip?" Cindy asked

"We are going to Nancy's first in Kentucky, I've got her phone number here and any other numbers you may need. We'll be staying there for a couple nights before we go on to

Louisiana. Nancy and her two children will be going with us down to Louisiana. From Nancy's it's about ten hours, give or take a little."

"What about the children? Are they going to the prison with you?" Cindy asked.

"The first day I'm going alone. The second day I'll take the kids with me."

Concerned, Cindy asked, "Are you sure it's safe?"

"Dakota says the kids and I will be more than safe. Cheryl and Rich have been there plenty of times. They have even taken their grandson to see Dakota. It can't be too bad if they did that."

"No, I guess not. I'm not sure I could do what you're doing. I think after watching T.V. so much I would be afraid I'd never get out," Cindy said with a slight laugh.

"I have had that thought cross my mind, but I know Dakota would never put us in harm's way. I really can't wait to see him. I just wish we could bring him home."

"Well, you have a safe trip and call me when you get back."

"I will. We're leaving at six in the morning. I've got the van all packed and the kids have their clothes all set out for the morning. It will be a great trip and one that we all need. See you later and thanks again."

Dawn gave Cindy a hug and was out the door. On her drive back home Dawn thought about the trip.

Chapter 14

Dakota was waiting outside the warden's office when the warden opened his office door. "Dakota, do you need to speak with me?"

"Yes Sir, Warden, if you have a minute."

"Come on in, Dakota."

Dakota got up from where he was sitting and walked into the warden's office. The warden had a big office. The desk was dark cherry with fancy carvings on it. He had a high-backed wing chair made of leather. Behind the warden's desk was a large picture window. The curtains were a deep burgundy pulled open by gold tasseled tiebacks. The walls were a medium brown paneling. The pictures on the wall were a few that Dakota had made the warden years ago.

"Sit down, Dakota. What can I do for you?" the warden said as he motioned for Dakota to sit down.

As he sat down from across the Warden, Dakota said, "Well Sir, My wife and children are coming down for a visit. I would like a special visit set up at the main camp."

"How long will she be down here?"

"She'd stay as long as she could if I'd let her, but I think a two-day visit is long enough," Dakota said smiling.

"Fine, I can arrange that. What do you think about a visit at the main camp visiting center? Or did you have a private visit in mind."

"No Sir! The main camp visiting center will be just fine. I want her to see me as an inmate. She has no idea of what I really am, and I intend to keep it that way," Dakota said.

"As you wish, Dakota."

As Dakota rose from his chair and started to walk towards the door, he turned around towards the warden.

"Warden."

"Yes Dakota?"

"One more thing."

"Yes."

"I don't want, under any circumstances for my wife to be strip searched. She is to be treated with respect by the guards. My children are not to be searched at all. Walking through the medal detector will be enough. They are not to be messed with, in any way," Dakota said firmly.

"I'll take care of it, Dakota."

"Thanks, Warden, I knew you would."

As the door closed behind Dakota, the warden let out a deep breath. Having a government agent living in the prison as an inmate could be hair raising at times. Dakota was a good man and had helped the warden and the prison out several times. Without Dakota living on the inside, the warden doubted if they would have received the governmental funds that they had.

The warden could understand why Dakota didn't want his wife and children subjected to the normal search. After all, Dakota wasn't just any inmate. The normal search would consist of the visitors being patted down and walking through a medal detector, like they use at the airports. Then the guards check them over with the wand if any of the detectors sounded the visitor would then be stripped searched to see if they were carrying any weapons into the prison system. Earrings, watches, and even a woman's under wire bra could set these off. With the kinds of inmates the prison had, the guards could not afford to be too careful. They had seen people trying to smuggle all kinds of things in. In places on the body most people wouldn't even dream of using.

Early that evening, Dawn's brother Mike called with good news. The army had changed their mind and Mike was getting his retirement two-months early. He wasn't going to Desert Storm after all. It looked like the house was going to sell and Mike and his family would be coming home.

Dawn was relieved and so happy. She told Mike that she was leaving the next day for her trip down to see Dakota. Mike told her to tell Dakota thanks and that he couldn't wait to meet him. Mike agreed with Dawn, that Dakota surely had a special connection with God. What other answer could there be?

After the children were all tucked into bed for the night, Dawn thought she'd take a long hot bath. As the water was running Dawn poured her bubble bath into the tub. She loved to soak in a hot tub and read a good romance. It was so relaxing. Then the phone rang. She reached over the edge of the tub and picked up the cordless.

"Hello," Dawn said.

"Good Evening, and how is my wife tonight?"

"Just sitting in my bubble bath reading a good romance, waiting for my knight in shining armor to call." She laughed.

"Oh yea, want me to wash your back?"

"Please, kind sir, would you? And while you're at it could I have a cup of coffee too?" Dawn teased him back.

"Yes Ma'am, coming right up. Will that be with one lump of sugar or two, or should I just shower you with kisses and skip the coffee?"

"Hmm, now that's a tough choice."

"Really now? Maybe I should just let you get back to your romance. Then you can call me later and tell me if it's as good as I am," Dakota teased her.

"I guess I could put it down for a little while and give you a whirl on romance. Then I'll compare notes later and see who's better," she said and they both laughed at that.

"That sounds fair to me. So what time are you leaving in the morning?"

"I thought around six, that way we can be to Nancy's no later than five. You know plan on bathroom breaks and such."

"Well, just take your time and be careful," he said.

"I will, don't worry."

"What way do you plan on taking down?"

As Dawn told Dakota the route she planned on taking Dakota was busy writing the information down.

"Your mom and Rich say this is the best way to go and the shortest."

"Sounds like a good game plan to me. I sure do miss you, honey."

Not meaning to let her feelings show in her voice, Dawn said, "I know the feeling, I miss you so much sometimes it hurts."

Hearing her voice like this, Dakota let his guard down unexpectedly, "Yes but we'll work through all of this. I've told you before, loving a man in prison isn't easy. Having you away from me and being on your own hurts me too. I need to be there with you and the children."

"In a few days we'll be there with you. I can't tell you how much I'm looking forward to that. I don't care where it's at Dakota, just to be with you means the world to me."

"Someday, somehow, someway, we'll be together. Then we won't have to worry about it," Dakota said with sadness to his voice. Dawn knew it was time to change the subject. They were both getting a little down.

"Guess who called a few hours ago? My brother. The Army has come to their senses and is giving him his retirement, after all. Dakota, you surely must have a hot line to the Lord. You were right when you said everything would be ok."

"That's great honey." Dakota thought to himself, *"If it wasn't for the Lord he just might not have his connections."*
"So, I guess, this means he won't be going to Desert Storm after all?"

"No, Dakota, I just can't thank you enough. Mike says to tell you thanks too. He can't wait to meet you."

"I'm just glad it all worked out. So, are the children excited about the trip?"

"Yes, I thought they'd never go to sleep. They're all wound up about it," Dawn said with a yawn.

"Speaking of sleep, I think I'd better let you get out of that tub before you turn into a prune. You need your rest."

"I'm fine, Dakota. Really, I am."

"Honey, I know that someday we will have wrinkles, and I'll love you just the same, but let's not push it," he teased her.

"You're something, Mr. Deer."

"Yes I am, Mrs. Deer, now tell me good night."

"Good night, I love you."

"And I love you, Mrs. Deer."

With that he was gone. Dawn put the phone down and rinsed off. Once she dried off she got ready for bed.

Lying in her bed, Dawn thought about Dakota, and fell asleep. She dreamed of the day he would come home and how he would surprise her.

Little did Dawn know that she wouldn't be going on this trip alone. Several agents would be going with her and she would never know that they were there. It wouldn't be the same agents all the time, Dakota had made arrangements that they would trade off every four hours. This way Dawn would never suspect she was being followed. There would even be agents at the prison posing as prison inmates and prison guards.

Dawn reached over to hit the off button on the alarm. She was surprised when it didn't turn off. She tapped it again but the noise continued. She then pulled on the clock and yanked the cord out of the wall, but the noise still continued. Dawn sat up in bed, finally realizing it wasn't the clock at all but the phone ringing. She stumbled over to the phone and picked it up. "Hello," she said half awake.

"Good morning Darling, this is your wake up call," Dakota said knowing this phone call would surprise her.

"Dakota?"

"Yes Ma'am, it's me. You must have been sound asleep. I thought you'd never answer the phone."

"I thought it was the alarm and even though I shut it off, it wouldn't stop. Then I realized it was the phone." She'd never tell him how she jerked the alarm clock cord out of the wall.

"Better get your coffee made honey, sounds like you could use it," he said sweetly.

"What time is it Dakota?" she asked still hanging on to the alarm clock cord.

"Four-thirty a.m. I thought I'd have coffee with you before you got the children up."

"Hang on a minute, I'll be right back."

Dawn started her coffee, ran to the bathroom, brushed her teeth, and washed her face with cold water. When she picked up the phone again, she felt a little more awake.

"Ok, I'm back."

"I thought maybe you had changed your mind and went back to bed, leaving poor Dakota here hanging," he laughed.

"Guess I could have, it wouldn't be the first time you listened to me sleep on the phone," Dawn said.

One time Dakota had called Dawn around seven in the evening. He had talked to all the children and even helped Dawn tuck them into bed, the best he could over the phone. Then Dakota and Dawn talked until midnight when Dawn fell asleep with the phone to her ear. Dakota listened to Dawn as she slept. It wasn't long and Dakota fell asleep too. Around five the next morning Dakota woke up and started talking to Dawn to wake her up. As she woke up, she was embarrassed that she had fallen asleep while talking to Dakota. When the children woke up, they found Dawn still on the phone with Dakota. Leigh had teased Dakota and said that sleeping on the phone would be expensive. "Dakota you must really love Mom. I'd never pay to listen to someone sleep." Dakota had told Leigh that people in love did silly things. And then Dakota's voice brought Dawn back to the present. "Yea well the next time I sleep with you, I'll be in the same bed," Dakota teased Dawn."Oh you will, will you? Just make sure you don't hog all the blankets. I get cold easy," Dawn teased back.

"Honey, you'll never be cold with me. I'll keep you as snug

as a bug, you can count on that. I just wanted to call and make sure you were wide awake before starting on your trip."

"I'm getting there, a few more cups of coffee and I'll be fit as a fiddle."

"I'm not going to keep you on the phone long, I know you have last minute things to do. I'll see you in a few days. Tell the kids I love them and I'm looking forward to seeing them," he said.

"I will, I love you."

"I love you Mrs. Deer, you be careful."

"You know I will, Dakota."

"Get off the phone Darling, so you can get here to see me sooner."

"Good-bye Dakota." With that she hung up the phone.

Dawn finished her coffee and woke the children up. "Good morning sleepy heads. Let's get ready so we can get started on our trip." Three children flew out of bed. They were excited about the trip.

"Where's Lou?" Dawn asked.

"She's still in bed, Mom," Lynn said.

As Dawn walked into the bedroom there was Lou still sleeping with her doll. Dawn kneeled down next to the bed, took her finger and lightly caressed Lou's face. "Wake up sleepy head. We've got a big day ahead of us." Lou opened her eyes and smiled at her mom. "Mom, I'm still tired."

"I know baby-girl, you were born tired. You can go back to sleep in the van if you want to," Dawn said softly.

Lou smiled at Dawn. She loved it when her mom told her she was born tired, and sometimes Lou wondered if it wasn't true. She was always the first one to bed and the last one up.

Reaching her hand out to her mom, Dawn took Lou's hand and helped her out of bed. "Let's put your baby doll in your suitcase. Then you'll have her with you on the trip." They put the doll in the suitcase and Lou was now excited about the trip.

After breakfast when the dishes were done, everyone was

ready to leave for their trip. The suitcases were taken out to the van. Dawn had packed a box of coloring books, hand-held games, cards, and books for the children.

A few nights before the trip Dawn and the children had highlighted the roads they would take on the trip with a yellow marker in the road atlas. This way the children could follow along on the maps of each state and know where they were.

"I'll be the pilot and each of you will take turns and be my co-pilot. It will be your job to tell me when I have to change roads," Dawn had told them. The children loved doing this. Dawn felt that learning to read a map was good for them. No one was ever too young to learn.

Chapter 15

Just before leaving Dawn checked to make sure her hidden keys on the van were in place. She had one up under the front bumper, one inside the gas door and one on the frame of the van. This way if she locked her keys in the van or lost them, she still had another set.

After a few hours on the road they decided to stop and stretch their legs for a few minutes. They were in Indiana at the time. The weather was warm and the sun was out. It was a great day for a trip. The children were having a good time.

It was getting to be lunchtime and so Dawn pulled into the next McDonald's. The children ordered Happy Meals and were excited about the toys inside the boxes. They ate their lunches and played in the McDonald's Funland for about an hour.

Once back on the road, the children and Dawn were singing happily to the country music playing on the radio. Once in awhile they would all stop singing to listen to what the truckers on the CB were saying. They all had their own handles and would sometimes talk to the truckers.

Early that evening, they pulled into Nancy's. Everyone was excited. Nancy and her children ran out of the house to greet them. Everyone was hugging everyone else. It had been a year since they had all seen each other.

The six children went out back to play while Nancy and Dawn went into the house and had coffee.

"So how was your trip?" Nancy asked Dawn.

"It was great, good weather all the way, and not too much traffic."

"My fiancé, Jerry, will be over later after he gets out of work."

"I'm really looking forward to meeting him. What does he think about you and the kids going with us to Louisiana?"

"He thinks it's a fine idea, but wonders why you're in love with a man in prison. He says he'd like to introduce you to a good ole southern gentleman, but understands the quest you're on. He says if you ever change your mind, he'll fix you right up."

"That sounds like the Jerry I've talked to on the phone," Dawn said with a laugh. "So when are the two of you tying the knot?"

"We're not sure yet, maybe sometime this fall. Thought maybe you'd like to come back down and be my maid of honor."

"I'd love it. It will be great to see you happily married. What do your parents think of Jerry?"

"Mom and Dad just love him. He fits right into our family. Jerry and Dad like to hunt and fish together. He's kinda the son my dad never had."

"That's great Nancy. I know Jimmy and Angela think the world of Jerry. They say he's a great dad."

"I know, who would have ever guessed after Doyle was killed in that car accident six years ago that I would one day meet someone like Jerry. I guess moving from Michigan after the accident and down here closer to Mom and Dad was the right thing to do."

"I'm so happy for you, Nancy. Jimmy and Angela seem to love Kentucky also. They tell me that they ride their grandpa's horses."

"Yes, my dad has fixed up a wagon for Jimmy and his wheel chair and Angela does really well riding bare back. We'll go out to the farm while you're here. The kids will just love all the animals they have."

"Sounds like fun to me."

"So what do you hear from Tom, anything?"

"Not since the divorce. He'll send the kids cards on their birthdays and at Christmas, but other than that nothing."

"Does it seem to bother them that they don't see him?"

"Not at all, I think they're afraid that he will treat them as he treated me. I was sure happy the judge didn't allow any visitation."

"I remember how Tom treated you. When I lived up in Michigan by you, I was always worried Tom would someday kill you. When I left Michigan and moved here to Kentucky I prayed that someday you would leave that asshole."

"Well I used to call you and tell you that I was going to. Other than you and my sister Marie, no one knew I was leaving him."

"Did I ever tell you that he called me down here and wanted to know if you and the kids were here?"

"Did he?"

"Yes, I think it was about a week after you left him. He must have got my phone number off one of the old phone bills. Anyway, I acted shocked and told him I couldn't believe you'd leave. He bought everything I said. He really must have thought I was stupid or something like I didn't know that he beat you. The best thing you ever did was to leave that jerk."

"You've got that right! I've never been happier in my life."

"I've got supper about ready. I hope you and the kids are hungry, I've cooked enough to feed an army."

"It smells really good, what are you cooking?"

"Possum stew and biscuits," Nancy said with a smile.

The look on Dawn's face said it all. Nancy couldn't hold back any longer, she started to laugh, "I'm only teasing, I haven't turned hillbilly all the way yet. It's venison stew."

The relieved look on Dawn's face made Nancy laugh all the more. Then Dawn started to laugh. "I thought for a minute there I was at ole Jed Clampett's and that Granny was doing the cooking."

Later that evening after supper was over, Nancy and Dawn took a walk with the kids to the park. It was a small town. When they would walk by houses with people sitting on their front porches, they would call out to Nancy and Dawn's little group, "Evening, right pretty evening for a walk."

"I can see why you enjoy Providence so much. It's small, quiet and everyone is so friendly," Dawn said.

"Yea, and it's safe. Everyone watches out for each other. The southern people have really taken to Jimmy. They don't see his wheel chair, just Jimmy for the kid he is. Dawn, you wouldn't believe how he's all over town, just like any other kid his age. Up north I would have never dreamed of letting him out of my sight, but down here it's a whole new world."

"I know when I'm down here I feel real relaxed and content," Dawn said.

"Maybe you should think about moving down here. The schools are good, the cost of living is cheap, and there are plenty of jobs." Nancy was giving her sales pitch to Dawn again.

"Believe me, Nancy, the thought has crossed my mind lately more than once. It's one of the things I want to talk with Dakota about."

"Dakota? I thought he was from Michigan."

"He is, but this would put me only ten hours away from him and I could go down and see him more often. The children and I would be happy here. We'd be close to you, and only ten hours from home, so we could still go up and see family on weekends. We'd be right in the middle of everyone we love."

"When we get back from Louisiana, we can start looking for a house. Might take most of the summer, but I know we can find something for you," Nancy said.

As they walked into the park, a ball game was going on. They sat up in the bleachers and watched while the children went to the playground.

After the game was over they walked back to Nancy's and found Jerry there baking cookies.

"Something smells good," Jimmy said.

"Ya know Jimmy, I thought to myself, what would six kids want when they got home from a long walk with two old fogy women?"

"Chocolate chip cookies!" Jimmy answered him.

"With chocolate milk to dunk them in," Angela said.

"The six of you kids pull up a chair and sit down. I've got some warm cookies waiting for you."

As the children got all settled with their cookies and milk, Nancy introduced each child and Dawn to Jerry.

"Ladies, I also have something for you." Jerry walked to the refrigerator and pulled out a couple of wine coolers for Nancy and Dawn and a beer for himself.

"Lets go sit on the porch for a spell and visit," Jerry said.

A half hour later, with their fill of cookies and milk, six sleepy children came out on the porch and said good night.

It was a warm night with a full moon and the stars seemed brighter than Dawn had seen in years. Sitting on the porch with Jerry and Nancy visiting was wonderful, Dawn thought.

The phone was ringing inside the house and Nancy went to answer it. She brought the phone out to Dawn. "There's a sexy southern gentleman on the phone for you, Miss Dawn."

"Really now? The only sexy southern gentleman I know who would be calling me here would be Dakota," Dawn said, taking the phone from Nancy.

"I do believe he did mention that was his name," Nancy said.

"Good Evening Miss Dawn, this is Mr. Dakota Deer and rumor has it I'm a very sexy southern gentleman."

"Oh are you now? Where did you hear something like that?" Dawn said smiling and looking at Nancy.

"Miss Nancy told me that, she said that if my voice was any indication of what I looked like, Miss Dawn was one lucky woman. So what do you think Miss Dawn? Are you a lucky woman?"

"Hmm... I'll have to ponder that one, Mr. Deer, I do believe I'll wait and see if it's in your kiss. Then I'll let you know."

"Trust me, honey, when I kiss you it'll be a kiss you'll never forget," Dakota said with just a little arrogance in his voice.

"Well Mr. Deer, do I detect just a little conceit in your voice?" Dawn teased.

"No brag Ma'am, just pure fact. So how was your trip?"

"No problems, the weather was just perfect and not much traffic on the roads."

"Are Nancy and the kids still coming with you?" he asked.

"Yes they are, they're all excited about it. We've booked a suite at the Saint Francis Ville Inn. The lady at the inn said she had all kinds of brochures on different things to see while we were there."

"That's great Honey, you just be sure to play tourist while you're here and have a good time."

"We will Dakota, but only after we've seen you. After all, seeing you is why we are coming."

"I'm going to let you go so you can visit with Nancy, but I'll see you in a few days. I love you Dawn, tell the kids I love them too."

"I love you, and I'll be sure to tell the kids."

"Good night, Darling."

"Good night, Dakota."

The next two days flew by as Nancy and Dawn caught up on all that had been happening since their last visit. They talked until early in the morning. The night before they left they had promised they would go to bed at a reasonable hour, so they wouldn't be tired for the trip.

The next morning as everyone piled into Dawn's van, they were thankful for its size. Dawn's van was a twelve-passenger van with straight windows. It had three bench seats, and the two-bucket seats in the front, giving plenty of room to the children. With everyone in the van they were at long last on their way to Louisiana.

As they traveled through the different states, Dawn and Nancy would take turns pointing out interesting things to the children. The children were in awe of the changing landscape and the different styles of homes they were seeing as they traveled.

The truckers were friendly and the children took turns talking to different ones along the way. Dawn wasn't sure who was having more fun on the CB, the truckers or the kids. The children explained to their listeners they were going to Louisiana to see their dad. Several of the truckers gave them the handle Six-Pack, just like the movie with Kenny Rogers in it, the truckers told the children. When the truckers found out that Dawn's dad was a truck diver too, they told the kids, "Well you know that means we're kinda family out here. We watch out for each other and our families who may be on the road. It's kinda like a special club," One truck driver explained. As they passed several trucks along the way, each truck driver would blow his air-horn and radio ahead that "the six-pack" was on the way.

The secret agents along on the trip also had CB's in their cars and were monitoring channel 19. They were enjoying the conversations, and even though they wouldn't admit it, wished they could join in. Following the women and children wasn't as boring as they thought it would be.

Dawn had no idea of the transmitter attached to her van, or the hidden bug in the van. It wasn't put there to invade Dawn's privacy, but as an added precaution for her safety. Dakota was taking no chances when it came to his family.

Hours later as they were crossing the Louisiana State line, everyone really perked up. "It's not far now and we'll be at our hotel," Dawn told them.

As they drove up the long driveway to the Saint Francis Ville Inn, the van was quiet. They were all in awe of the historical inn. It was a two-story mansion that had been converted into a hotel. The grounds were well groomed, with beautiful flowers everywhere. Spanish moss was hanging down the trees. It was as though they had stepped back in time. Nancy broke the silence, "Would you look at that? Dawn, this is wonderful, how did you find a place like this?"

"I didn't. Dakota told me about it. He said I wouldn't be disappointed, but I had no idea of how beautiful it would be."

Dawn parked the van and went in and checked on their room. When she returned to the van she said, "You won't believe it. Everyone's dressed in the civil war costumes. Wait till you see the inside!"

As they went in and were shown to their room, everyone was quiet as they took it all in. When the chambermaid opened their room for them, they were all speechless. The beds were tall four-poster beds with canopies, complete with stools for getting in and out of bed. The hand-made dressers had been restored. The love seat had fancy carvings on it. The curtains were made of velvet, and the walls had old time photos of the civil war, complete, with the old bubble glass and wooden frames. The lighting was old oil lamps, which had been made electric hanging on the wall, with a hurricane lamp on the table between the beds. The floors were hardwood, with homemade rugs scattered about. The only thing modern was the bathroom.

The chambermaid was use to this kind of reaction from tourists, but could never stop enjoying the pleasure on their faces. "My name is Darcy and if there be anything you'all be needing, please give me a holler and I'll do my best fer ya. Supper is between six and eight, breakfast is from five until seven-thirty, and lunch is served at twelve and ending at one-thirty. We have a wonderful pool and a lovely garden you may wish to stroll about. May I wish you all a good-evening.?" With that she smiled and left.

Nancy and Dawn just looked at each other, smiled, then at the same time each quickly climbed up on a bed, stretched out and said, "This is heaven." The children just laughed at them.

"Mom can we go swim in the pool?" Angela asked. The other children agreed it sounded like a wonderful idea.

"Maybe we should save that for tomorrow. I think we should go and eat supper now. What do you think, Dawn?"

"Supper sounds good to me. Dakota says everything here is homemade."

"We'll eat first, then lets check out the garden. Tomorrow can be kids day in the pool," Nancy said.

Knowing they were getting the better end of the deal, the children agreed. All day in the pool and only an hour or so walking around a silly garden tonight, was something they could live with.

After supper and a walk through the garden, the women could see the children were ready for bed. It had been a long event-filled day for everyone. After the six-pack was tucked in and fast asleep, Dawn and Nancy stepped out the back door of their room and sat on the porch. The porch ran the full length of the hotel. There were wicker chairs and tables outside of each room. On the outside wall, just above the table was a doorbell button with a sign above it that read. "If you would like an evening beverage please ring." Dawn looked at Nancy and said, "Now this is service above and beyond the call of duty."

"No Dawn, this is called, Southern Hospitality," Nancy said with a smile as she pushed the button.

Within three minutes a chambermaid appeared. "May I get you ladies something to drink?"

Dawn answered her, "Yes, could you please tell us what kind of pop you have?" The chambermaid gave Dawn a strange look and said, "Pop?"

Nancy quickly added, "What she means to say is, what kind of soda do you have?"

"Oh, soda. We have Coke, Mountain Dew, Pepsi, Root beer, and Orange Crush."

"We'll take a diet Coke and a diet Pepsi please."

"Yes Ma'am, I'll be back in a jiffy."

Dawn looked at Nancy, "A soda? It sounds like I'm wanting to bake."

"Yea, well she more than likely thought you were asking her

what kind of a father she had," Nancy said with a laugh. "Down South, Dawn, we call our fathers, Pop, and our Grandfathers Papee, or Papa. A good thing I've lived in the North and South. I understand how ya'll talk."

"Oh," Dawn said feeling embarrassed.

"Don't worry, we'll make a hillbilly out of you yet."

The next morning they all went to breakfast at the inn restaurant. When they were all seated Jimmy said, "Wow, can you smell that? Homemade sweet rolls."

"Mom, do you think I can have segettie?" Lou asked.

Nancy looked at Dawn, "Segettie?"

"Yes, Lou eats spaghetti anytime we go to a sit-down restaurant. She'd eat it three times a day if I'd let her."

"Lou, I don't think they serve it here in the morning, but we'll ask. If they don't then you can have it for lunch," Dawn said.

"Ok, Mom," Lou said hopping her mom was wrong.

When the waitress came, they all ordered and Lou found out that she'd have to wait until lunch for her spaghetti. So instead, she ordered scrambled eggs with lots of ketchup on them.

As they were all eating their breakfast, Dawn told her children that she was going to see Dakota today by herself.

"But Mom, that's not fair. We want to see him too! That's why we all came," Leigh said.

"You will see Dakota tomorrow, I just need to talk some adult things over with him today." That wasn't Dawn's real reason. She just needed to be sure that the prison was going to be a safe place for her children. "You can all swim in the pool today while I'm gone. After all we did make you the deal last night that you could swim all day today."

Nancy could see Dawn was needing help with this, "Yea, we'll have a blast in the pool. They even have a water slide and a diving board."

Leigh knew she wasn't going to get far with the adults. "Well you'd better take us tomorrow or Daddy Dakota will be really mad at you."

"I promise you'll go tomorrow," Dawn said.

When breakfast was done, they all returned to their room. The children and Nancy got ready for their day at the pool and Dawn got ready for her visit to the prison. When they were all ready they gathered their things and started towards the door. Leigh ran up to the door, put her back against it arms out and through tears said. "Mom, you can't leave without me. He's my Daddy and I want to see him too!"

As Dawn looked from Leigh to Nancy she said, "Nancy, why don't you take the kids to the pool. I need to talk to Leigh. We'll meet you there."

"Come on gang, let's hit the water," Nancy said.

Dawn took Leigh by the hand and walked over to the bed, sat down, and put her arms around Leigh. While the tears still ran down Leigh's face, Dawn said. "Honey, I know you love him too. I know you want to see him but Leigh; the real reason I want to go alone today is to make sure it's safe for you children. I've never been to a prison before and well, I just need to be sure."

Leigh's tears stopped and she looked up at Dawn and said, "Daddy Dakota wouldn't let us visit him, Mom, unless he knew we'd be safe. He told me that in a letter. 'Cause I asked him. Mom, are you scared?"

Dawn wasn't sure how to answer this, so she said, "Well kinda."

Leigh started to laugh, "So you think they're going to lock you up and not let you out?"

It was unnerving how this small child could read Dawn like a book. That's exactly what had crossed Dawn's mind, more than once. When Dawn didn't answer her, Leigh said. "Mom, are you chicken?"

"No, I'm not chicken, I just want to be sure."

"Sure Mom, you go today alone and when Daddy Dakota sees you didn't bring us, you're going to be in big trouble.

Tomorrow when I see Daddy Dakota, I'm telling him how you were afraid they'd lock you up," Leigh teased her mom. "Bet he'll ground you or something."

"Maybe. Are we ready to go to the pool now?"

"Yes, but I feel sorry for you, you're going to be in big trouble."

When they got to the pool Nancy asked Dawn if she was nervous. "Yes, I am. What if Dakota doesn't like the way I look? We haven't seen each other since we were teenagers."

"You've sent each other pictures haven't you?"

"Yes, tons of them."

"I don't think you have a thing to worry about. From the Dakota I've talked to and the way you make him sound, everything will be just fine."

Chapter 16

On her way to the prison Dawn remembered Dakota telling her not to speed and to watch the road. The road was long and very winding. On either side of the road were deep ditches, which Dakota had referred to as levee's, they were to keep the water off the road when the rains and flooding came. *"A semi could drive down there and no one would see it,"* Dawn thought to herself.

At the end of the road Dawn could see the prison gates and a small building. "That must be the visitor's shed that Dakota told me about," Dawn said to herself. She parked the van, removed her wallet from her purse, grabbed an unopened pack of cigarettes, took a deep breath and walked up to the door.

Looking the large room over as she walked in, Dawn noticed the counter Dakota had told her about. There were about five other women standing in line ahead of Dawn. As each woman ahead of Dawn checked in at the counter, they were patted down from top to bottom by a woman officer and then instructed to walk through the metal detector. When the alarms went off, Dawn jumped. Two officers gabbed the woman by her arms and took her to a room, the woman was yelling, "I ain't got nothing."

"Miss, may I help you?" The officers' voice captured Dawns attention. Dawn realized she was next in line at the counter.

"Yes, I'm here to see Dakota Deer."

"I.D. please." Dawn gave the officer her I.D. with the letter from the prison. As the officer typed the information into the computer a warning came up on the screen. Dawn Brown, wife of Dakota Deer, to be treated with KID GLOVES by order of the warden. Since she didn't know what the screen said, Dawn began to get worried that she wouldn't be allowed to see

Dakota.

The officer turned to Dawn, "Ma'am, I need to look in your wallet, and I'll need to open your cigarettes for you."

Dawn gave her wallet to the officer. The officer barely looked in her wallet but opened Dawn's cigarette pack, and put tape on the top of them. The officer then pushed a paper in front of Dawn and said, "Please sign this Ma'am, it's a document that will allow you to visit anytime during visiting days. Next time you visit all you will need to do is to show your I.D." Not even reading the form, Dawn signed it. She had no idea that she had just signed a visitor's form stating she was Inmate Dakota Deer's wife.

"Please step over to the next officer. She will pat you down, and then you'll go through the metal detector. From there you'll board the bus to go to the visiting center. We hope you enjoy your visit," the officer said.

"Thank you," Dawn said. Dawn stepped behind the lady in front of her and watched as the lady was patted down. Dawn was surprised that the lady didn't seem bothered by this at all. *"Must be she's been here to visit someone before?"* Dawn thought.

"Next," the lady officer said. Dawn walked up to the officer. The lady officer touched Dawn's ribs and said. "You may now go through the metal detector. Enjoy your visit."

"Thank you," Dawn answered with a puzzled look on her face. Not sure why she wasn't patted down as the others had been, but relived just the same, Dawn moved along. At the metal detector, the lady in front of Dawn removed her shoes before she walked through. Dawn couldn't see any metal on her shoes so she didn't understand why. As the lady walked through the alarm sounded. Another officer took the hand-held wand and scanned over the woman, again setting off the alarm. Two officers grabbed the women by her arms and took her to another room.

Dawn was dressed western style, with a blazer, long skirt

and cowboy boots. As Dawn came to the metal detector she started to remove her boots as she had seen others do before her. "Ma'am that won't be necessary," the officer stated.

"Oh, I just thought we all had to," Dawn replied.

"No Ma'am, please walk through."

As Dawn walked through, she held her breath, *"Why did I wear an under-wire bra today of all days?"* she thought to herself. When the alarm didn't go off, Dawn let out her breath. A woman guard on the other side said, "Would you please follow me. I'm the bus driver who will be taking you to the main prison visiting center. Is this your first visit?"

"Yes," Dawn said.

"Who are you here to see?" The guard could tell Dawn was tense and tried to get her to relax. She knew that Dawn was there to see Dakota Deer. If she was upset when she saw Dakota, there would be "hell to pay" by orders of the warden.

"Dakota Deer," Dawn replied.

"Inmate Deer, why he's one of the nicest men we have here. He's a good man and our top trustee. My name is Helen. If you have any questions, I'd be more than happy to answer them," Helen said with a smile.

"You know Dakota?" Dawn asked surprised.

"Yes Ma'am, you must be his wife. He talks about you all the time. Thinks the world of you and the children."

Helen could see Dawn was at ease now. "Watch your step Ma'am," she said as they boarded the bus.

The bus was blue and had bars on the windows and back door. The passengers were locked in the seating area by a barred wall that separated the passengers from the driver and the front door. Dawn looked at Helen. "We use this bus to move the inmates from camp to camp. It keeps them from attacking the driver. We also use it to transport visitors. There's no sense in spending tax payer's dollars for a separate bus. It also protects us from the visitors. You wouldn't believe what I've seen come in here." Helen also quickly added, "But mostly

119

it's just nice people like you coming in to see a loved one."

"Oh, I see," Dawn said.

The bus ride took about ten minutes. Dawn couldn't believe how big the prison grounds were. There were fields with inmates working them, and guards with shotguns on horse back watching over them. Dawn wondered if any of the inmates were ever shot while trying to escape but she wasn't about to ask. As they passed the fields, Dawn could see buildings ahead. Helen told Dawn that they were going to the main camp, where the visiting center was.

When they pulled up to the visiting center, Helen got off the bus and the other guard on the bus unlocked the cage. The other passengers were up and moving off the bus. Dawn was the last person off the bus. She followed the others into the building. Once in the building, the outside doors were locked. They were in a large room with a u-shaped counter, divided down the middle by a wall of bars. To the left was a barred door going into another room with plenty of tables and chairs.

"The inmates come in from the other side of the desk and bars," Helen told Dawn. "The visitors go through here. Once you're in the visiting room, feel free to sit at any table. Inmate Deer will then be brought in. Don't worry, you're really safe here."

"Thank you, I'm not worried. I'm just excited about seeing Dakota."

"You enjoy your visit, Ma'am."

Dawn picked a table at the back of the room next to the wall. This way she could see everyone around her and no one could sneak up on her.

As the inmates were being brought in to find their visitors, Dawn noticed they had handcuffs on them. Some of the inmates' handcuffs were removed once in the visiting room. Other's had their handcuffs left on. Most of the men had no laces in their boots, and a few were wearing loafers with no socks. Most of the inmates were seated but Dawn didn't see

Dakota. Five minutes went by with Dawn was still watching the inmate door, before long the door opened and out walked Dakota. Dawn noticed that he had no handcuffs and none had been removed. He had on a blue western cut shirt that had red embroidery on it, with new blue jeans, a wide leather belt with a fancy belt buckle, and cowboy boots on. Finally he had a wallet in his back pocket, attached by a chain to his belt.

His walk was steady and proud. *"Why is he dressed so different from the others?"* Dawn thought.

Dawn stood up as Dakota approached the table, smiling. When he reached her, he put his arms around her and held her like he'd never let her go. Laying her head on his shoulder, Dawn's arms went around him as the tears welled up in her eyes. Dakota whispered into her ear. "Mrs. Deer, have I told you that I love you yet today?" Looking up at Dakota and smiling through her tears she answered him, "No, not until now." Taking his arms from around her Dakota gently wiped the tears off her cheeks. "Honey, if you don't stop doing that the levee's going to overflow and everyone here will blame Dakota for being mean to his wife." Dawn laughed and she kissed Dakota and said, "Well we can't have that now can we? I love you, Dakota."

As they seated themselves at the table, Dakota asked Dawn, "Where's the kid's? I thought you were bringing them with you."

"They're at the hotel with Nancy. I wanted to come alone today. Guess you could say I was being selfish."

"And maybe Mom was checking things out to be sure the kids would be safe in a prison?" he asked. How well he knew her, Dawn thought.

"Well, that too," she said shyly.

"That's one of the things I love about you Dawn, the way you take care of those kids. How was your trip? What do you think about the hotel?"

"It was great, and the hotel is wonderful. They treat

everyone like royalty," she said sounding happy.

"Good, I'm glad you like it. Look, I've got a special visit so we can visit for four hours today and tomorrow. Most of the time inmates are only allowed a two-hour visit twice a month, but since you're from out of state, I asked for a longer visit to be granted."

"Oh, Dakota, that's great. I thought I was only going to see you two hours today and two hours tomorrow. Dakota, I really need to tell you something."

"What's that, Honey?"

"When I went through the visitors shed, they didn't even pat me down. Oh the lady touched my ribs, but that was all. Then when I went through the metal detector they didn't even have me take off my boots. The other ladies had to take off their shoes and some of them, were even taken to another room. Dakota, am I going to get into trouble here?" she sounded concerned.

Smiling Dakota said, "No Honey, you're not, they treated you that way, because of who you're here to see."

"Who I'm here to see?" she said looking confused.

"Dawn, they know I don't mess with drugs or weapons, and I'm not about to put anyone on my visitor's list who would try to smuggle that kind of contraband in here. I'm the most trusted man of over five thousand inmates in this prison. They know I'm not going to blow my chance of ever getting out of here by putting someone on my list who would bring that in."

"Is that also why the other inmates are dressed different from you? Most of them don't even have shoe laces in their boots, and some of them still have handcuffs on? Then you walk in and the guards act like you own the place," she said.

"It's because of, who I am," he answered Dawn.

"Oh," Dawn said. She wanted to ask more questions, but decided not to push the issue. Dawn changed the subject by commenting on his embroidered shirt. "Someone really did a nice job on your shirt."

"Thanks, it took me awhile, but I think it came out all right too."

Surprised and touching his shirt She said, "You did this?"

"Yea, it's not like we can send it out to have it done. We are in prison if you want something nice done around here, you have to do it yourself," Dakota said proudly.

"A good thing you know how because that's not my cup of tea. Do you darn your own socks too?" she asked with a laugh.

"No, I just throw them away. Why, do you want me to send them to you so you can darn them for me?"

"I sew as little as possible. So if you think sending them to me will do you any good, you might end up like some of these other inmates with no socks at all," she teased him.

Dakota leaned over and kissed Dawn on her cheek. "Honey, you're really cruel to make poor old Dakota go sockless. I'll be right back." Dakota walked over to the counter where they served food and beverages. He brought back two sodas.

He brought back, a diet Mountain Dew for Dawn and a diet Coke for himself. Sitting back down, Dakota took Dawn's hand and said, "I know the first ring I sent you didn't make it. It was one of my favorite rings. I made another one just like it and I want you to take it home with you." As he took the ring off his smallest finger, he explained to Dawn how he had made it. "The silver is from Europe and the turquoise is from North Dakota."

"Dakota, it's so pretty, I don't know, are you sure?" she said looking at the ring.

"Darling, several people have offered to buy this ring and the first one. Even my ma tried to talk me out of it, but being my favorite ring I wouldn't give it up. Now I want you to have it so you will know my heart is with you, my wife. He slipped the ring on Dawn's left ring finger, but it was a little too big. Dakota took it off and placed it on her middle finger. It was a good snug fit over the knuckle but loose enough behind it. "I guess this is all right for now I'll just have to make you a silver

wedding band, when I come home. I'll bring it with me."
Dawn's bottom lip began to quiver and tears welled up in her eyes. Dakota pulled Dawn gently over to him, and setting her on his lap, he put his arm around her and held her left hand. "Mrs. Deer, when I was younger I thought I knew what love was, like most young people, but living the life I have for the past fifteen years has taught me that true love only comes once in a life time. You, my Darling lady, are the love I have been waiting for." With that he gently kissed her.

The guards at the front of the room had been watching Dakota and Dawn. Helen said to Tim, "I've been here for ten years and never have I seen two people more in love."

"Yea, I know what you mean. It's too bad Dakota's got life. That girl's going to end up with a broken heart the size of Louisiana."

"Maybe," Helen said. "But I have a feeling those two will wind up together someday."

"I hope you're right, Helen. Dakota's a good man and deserves a second chance," Tim said. Helen said no more to Tim, but thought to herself, *"Tim, if you only knew the real story behind Dakota Deer."* She smiled at the thought.

"So tell me Darling, do you think I'm a man worth waiting for?" Dakota asked Dawn.

"I'd wait for you until the end of time and then some. I just wish I could take you home with us now."

"I'd love to go with you, when the time is right we'll be together and this will all be behind us. In the end, Dawn, this will only make our love stronger. I know that men have treated you badly in the past. Free men don't know how precious love is. They take a special woman like you for granted. I will never do that, being in a place like this has taught me just how serious life is. One day Mrs. Deer, you will be shown the happiness that two people like us deserve. Until then, know that wherever you go and whatever you do, my love is with you." And then he kissed her.

"Inmate Deer to the front," the voice said over the intercom.

Dawn gave Dakota a worried look. "It's all right. I'll be right back." Getting off of Dakota's lap, Dawn sat down in her chair at the table. She watched as Dakota talked to the guards at the counter in the front of the room.

"Inmate Deer check in please," Helen said to Dakota as she pushed the clipboard to him.

"Yes Ma'am," Dakota said as he signed in.

"Inmate Deer, I just want you to know I think you have a very nice wife," Helen said.

Dakota turned to look back at Dawn, then looking at Helen he said. "Yes Ma'am, She's one special lady."

"Well you enjoy the rest of your visit."

"Thank You Ma'am, I will," Dakota said. He then turned and walked back to Dawn. As he approached her, he could see the concerned look on her face.

As he sat down at the table, he took Dawn's hand in his. "At random they will call out an inmates name to check in. It's no big deal, just their way to show the state on paper that they keep track of us, during visits."

"I thought maybe they were going to take you back and I wouldn't even get to say goodbye," Dawn said concerned.

"I'm not going anywhere for a while," he said with a smile, and then continued, "Honey, you will never see them drag Dakota from you. There will always be time for me to tell you I love you, and hug and kiss you before I go."

Dakota knew when tomorrow's visit ended it was going to be rough on Dawn to leave. They, would deal with that then, but for now he was going to enjoy every moment with her. Sometimes they would just sit and not even talk, just being together and holding hands was an intimacy most people would never understand. It was the nineties and most people based love on the physical aspects of a relationship, forgetting that friendship and love of the heart must come first for true love to endure.

They talked about the children, how school was going, and the children's trip to the radio station. Dawn had sent Dakota pictures of the children at the radio station in the D.J.'s booth. Complete with headsets on, they were pretending to talk into the microphone as if they were actually transmitting over the air.

One Halloween, Dawn went to the school and recorded several of the children giving a safety message to other children. They would say their name, what school they were from and then their safety message for Halloween. The tape was then played over the air the day of Halloween. Dawn had copied this tape for Dakota and sent it to him. They talked about that, and how cute all the children sounded.

They talked about the house they would have someday. It was to be a large farmhouse with lots of bedrooms, a pole barn to house a wood shop, way out in the country so the children could run and explore.

Dakota teased Dawn that he'd never let them starve. "I'm an awesome hunter, if he walks out in front of me, he's mine."

"You know, I just may hold you to that. Wild meat is so much better."

"Yes Ma'am, the turkey, rabbits and the big bucks will be filling your freezer when I get home. I might even add a few fish, just for variety." He smiled at her.

"As long as you leave the possum, rattlesnake, and the alligators down south that will be just fine."

"I don't eat possums, but rattlesnake and alligator are pretty good. It's something you should try while down here." And then he winked at her.

Dawn wrinkled her face, "I don't think so, southern boy, I'll pass."

"All right, but it's a lot like snapping turtle and frog legs, and you like them."

"This is true, but my dad had us eating that since we were young. So I wasn't old enough to know better and by the time

I was old enough, I didn't care what it was, I just enjoyed it."

"Well if you change your mind, let me know and I'll bring some home with me."

"Save yourself the packing room and eat up while you still can," she teased him back.

When their time was up, Dakota walked Dawn to the front of the room. "I'll see you tomorrow. Tell the children I'm looking forward to seeing them."

"I will. I love you."

He drew her into his arms and kissed her, "I love you."

As Dawn started to walk away to follow Helen back to the bus, Dakota said, "Dawn." She turned and looked at Dakota. "Yes," she said.

"Try the snake tonight at the inn. I hear it's really superb." He smiled.

Dawn stuck her tongue out at him and made no reply. Dakota let out a good hearty laugh as she smiled back at him.

On the bus ride back to the visitor's shed Dawn was thinking about the day she had, with Dakota. She was glad that she hadn't brought the children. She needed today alone with Dakota. Tomorrow will be a family day.

The pool was full of swimmers and Dawn didn't even notice Nancy or the children. She was daydreaming of Dakota.

"Hey Mom," Leigh called out Dawn turned her head towards the familiar voice. "How's Daddy Dakota, are they being good to him?"

"He's doing great, he can't wait to see you tomorrow."

"Did you get grounded? Must be Daddy told them to let you out," Leigh said as she climbed out of the pool.

"No, I didn't get grounded, and yes must be they let me out, as you can see I'm standing here."

"Not to be disrespectful Mom, but kinda looks to me that I trusted Dad more than you did," Leigh said.

"In my defense Miss Leigh, all I can say is I was being that over protective parent again," Dawn said as she tousled Leigh's hair.

"I guess we'll let you off this time Ma'am, just don't try it again tomorrow," Leigh said, shaking her head so water would fly on Dawn.

"Hey, you know, sugar melts!" Dawn grabbed Leigh and threw her back into the pool. When Leigh came back up, she was laughing. Dawn's children swam like fish and loved it when Dawn would throw them in. Leigh was pretending to be the mean witch in the Wizard of Oz, "You bad little girl, look what you've done to me, I'm melting, I'm... m-e-l-t-i-n-g..."

"Go swim little mermaid, in a little while we're going to eat," Dawn said as she waved at Leigh. Then Dawn walked over to where Nancy was sitting. "Want some coffee?" Nancy asked.

"Sounds great."

"You look tired. How was Dakota?"

"He's great, just great. I really hated to leave him there. I'm so in love with him Nancy, I don't know what I'll do if he never gets out," Dawn said as she sipped the coffee Nancy gave to her.

"So what's this big thing on your finger?" Nancy asked pointing to Dawn's hand.

"Remember when I had told you that Dakota was sending me a ring from prison and it got lost in the mail? Well he made another one just like it, only to fit his pinky finger, hoping it would fit mine and he gave it to me."

"Wow, that's really pretty. I knew by the video that you brought down and that we watched he was talented, but there was never a good close up of the rings he made. He's some kind of artist, in more than one area. That man will spoil you rotten someday," Nancy said in awe.

"Maybe, but I'm after the man, not the artist."

"Oh I know that, but might as well have both."

"Once he's home, I don't care what he does, as long as we're together. So how were the fish today?"

"Swimming in schools. It won't be long before they'll be wrinkled like old men and women. They should be pretty close to water logged by now. Shall we call them out and feed the fish, or just throw the food into the tank?" Nancy asked.

"I don't know, shall we ask them? It might be easier to throw it to them," Dawn said and then they both laughed.

In the room the children were changing clothes and asking where they were going to eat. When all six were asked what they wanted, McDonald's was the only answer Nancy and Dawn got.

At McDonald's the children ate and then went and played in the Funland, leaving Dawn and Nancy to finish their coffee and talk.

"They'll be out like lights tonight," Nancy said to Dawn.

"Won't it be great? I can't thank you enough Nancy for coming with us. It meant the world to me to be alone with Dakota today."

"Don't thank me, I'm getting a vacation out of this. I have to tell Jerry about the inn. What a great place for a honeymoon."

"It would be, wouldn't it? Maybe Dakota and I will stay there someday."

"So how was the prison?" Nancy asked.

"I've never seen anything like it in my life. I rode on an inmate bus, we were locked in, but there were no inmates on it, just visitors going to the visiting center. They had inmates working in the fields with guards on horseback watching them. In the visiting center inmates came in with no laces in their boots, no belts, and some were even in handcuffs. Before Dakota came in and after seeing all the other inmates I wondered if they would have him in handcuffs, since he is in prison for first degree murder."

"So tell me how did he look?"

"Hansom of course, and you'll never believe this! He was dressed in new jeans, a western shirt, wide leather belt with a fancy belt buckle, cowboy boots, and get this, a leather wallet with a chain attached to his belt. Walked right in like he owned the damn place," Dawn said still amazed by it and then she continued. "The guards treated him with respect. Hell when he got up to go to the bathroom they even opened the door for him, like he was some kind of royalty or something. They didn't do that for the other inmates. I just don't understand it."

Looking puzzled at Dawn, Nancy said, "That just doesn't sound right."

"I know it didn't look right either. I never would have believed it if I hadn't seen it with my own eyes. Then again, the video of him in prison isn't normal either," Dawn said.

"You're telling me. My uncle is in prison and he doesn't live in a ranch house, have horses, and never would they allow him to train drug dogs and work with the cops. Then you take Dakota's wood shop in that video, hell Dawn, if I remember that video right; Dakota wasn't dressed like an inmate in that either. I've been to see my uncle and he's always been dressed in prison clothes. Something's not right here," Nancy said shaking her head.

"Yea, but what? Dakota says it's because of who he is. He tells me it's because they know he's not going to mess with drugs or weapons and they know he's working to get out of there."

"So is my uncle and he's not even in for murder. I think there's more to this story then you'll ever know. You're down south and it's a different world here. It's not like Michigan. They can do anything they want down here."

"Good, maybe that means Dakota is right and he'll really get out someday." Dawn smiled.

"Wouldn't surprise me, not the way you say they treated him and all."

Once back at the hotel with the children all tucked into bed, Nancy and Dawn sat on the porch and enjoyed the evening. A waitress had brought Nancy and Dawn their evening sodas and was walking towards them with a cordless phone in her hand.

"Ma'am, you have a phone call. When your done, ring the bell and I'll come get the phone. Have a nice evening," she said as she handed Dawn the phone.

"Thank you," Dawn said and gave Nancy a questioning look.

"Hello."

"Good Evening Darling."

"Dakota?"

"Were you expecting someone else?" he teased.

"Oh sure, I have all kinds of inmates calling me from prison at a hotel," Dawn teased back.

"Really now? I'll have to talk to the warden about that. I just called to see how much trouble Mom got into with the children for not bringing them today."

"Leigh thinks you should ground me, but the others were fine and gave me no problem. You can count on Leigh telling you all about it tomorrow. She was fine when I got back, but I'm sure she won't forget to let you know how mad she was at me," Dawn said.

"That's my girl, keeping Mom on the straight and narrow. Bet she won't let you leave tomorrow without them," he laughed.

"No, I guess not. Lucky for me I'm bringing them."

Dakota knew Dawn was still concerned for the children's safety, "Good, cause I'd hate to have to ground you. I'm really looking forward to seeing them. Don't worry Mom, they'll be safe here."

"I'm not. I just needed to see you alone today, that's all," she fibbed.

"Honey, you haven't seen me alone yet, but when you do, you'll never want to leave."

"Promises, promises, promises."

"No Ma'am, just fact. I'm going to let you go and I'll see you in the morning. I love you Darling."

"I love you. Goodnight Dakota." And Dawn hung up the phone.

"I take it that was Dakota? Isn't it amazing how he can call you anytime day or night?" Nancy said as she gave Dawn a strange look.

"What do you mean?"

"Like I told you, this whole thing is strange. My uncle is only allowed to call on certain days and certain hours. They are only allowed to talk ten to fifteen minutes, and they can only call collect. Dakota doesn't call you collect, and you can well bet they don't have calling cards in prison."

"I know he's really not an inmate. He's just living there at the prison because he likes it. Hell maybe he's working for the prison but doesn't want his family to know. Better yet, he really loves me, but just can't pull himself away from the Holiday Inn, you know room service and all," Dawn said laughing.

"Well really what I had in mind was that he's a spy, you know like 007, trying to catch the bad guys."

Dawn was laughing so hard at this that she was doubled over. When she was able to stop laughing, she said, "That shouldn't be too hard, they are all bad guys in prison. Won't be long and the warden will figure that out and 007 Dakota will be without a job." Nancy and Dawn laughed a little while longer, and then decided they should turn in for the night.

The next morning when Dawn and the children were ready to leave for the prison, Lynn ran into the bathroom.

"Lynn, are you all right?" Dawn could hear her throwing up. She walked into the bathroom. "I'll get you a warm washcloth." Handing the washcloth to Lynn as she finished, Dawn felt her forehead. There seemed to be no fever. Dawn wondered what could be wrong.

"Do you hurt anywhere?" Dawn asked.

"No, I was feeling just fine until a minute ago. Maybe you and the other kids should go, without me, Mom," Lynn said looking a little pale.

"Lynn, I don't want to leave you behind. We can only see Dakota today, otherwise you won't get to see him at all this trip."

"I can stay with Aunt Nancy. She won't mind." Dawn sensed that maybe Lynn was nervous. Maybe she was afraid to go to the prison. Dawn didn't want to pressure her into going.

"If you're sure, I don't want you to feel like we left you out."

"No Mom, you go ahead and go. Tell Dakota that I love him and I'll see him next time."

Dawn looked at Nancy, who had overheard the conversation. Nancy nodded her head at Dawn and whispered, "She was nervous about it all day yesterday. Leave her here, she'll be fine."

Giving Lynn a hug and telling her she'd see her later, they left. The drive to the prison took about twenty minutes. The kids were excited and every five minutes would ask Dawn, "Mom, are we almost there?"

Chapter 17

Pulling into the parking lot and seeing the guard towers and the visitors shed the children became quiet. Scott then spoke up. "Wow, would you look at that, it's just like on T.V." "Yes it looks that way, but this is real. Now you all know what I expect..." Dawn said.

Right on cue, the children finished the saying that Dawn had taught them, "Nothing but angels, absolute angels and you will accept nothing less."

"That's right." Dawn smiled at them. "Let's go in, and be polite."

Once in the visitors shed, the children went right into "Angel" mode. They checked in and the guards thought they were so cute. They weren't patted down and all walked through the metal detector and then boarded the bus.

Helen thought the children were adorable and asked them their names. They answered Helen, and then politely sat in their seats. Leigh sat with Scott and Dawn sat with Lou, across the isle. Once Helen took a count of the visitors on the bus she sat down and they were on their way.

As they approached the visiting center, Leigh started looking for Dakota. "Mom, are you sure he's going to be here today?"

"Leigh, he wouldn't miss seeing you kids for the world." Leigh turned her head and started looking for him as the bus came to a stop.

Walking into the visiting center the children noticed the bars and knew it was to keep anyone from leaving without permission. Sitting at a table, the children watched for Dakota as the inmates started to come in.

Leigh's back was towards the front of the room so she turned in her chair to watch for him. When Dawn spotted

Dakota she said, "There he is."

Looking back at her mom, Leigh said, "Mom that's not Daddy Dakota. That man's too good looking."

"Oh you think so? I'll be sure to tell him you said that, but that's him, Leigh. Watch and see if that man doesn't come right up to us."

When Dakota reached the table he bent down and kissed Dawn and Leigh's face turned red.

"And why are you blushing so?" Dakota asked Leigh. Jumping up out of her chair, Leigh went over and hugged Dakota. Lou followed and crawled up on his lap. Scott being a polite young man walked over and offered his hand for a hand shake. Dakota looked over the girl's heads and smiled at Dawn and said to Scott, "Well hello, Son." Dakota shook his hand and pulled him over for a family hug.

"Where's Lynn?" Dakota asked.

"She got sick this morning," Lou answered.

"She's back at the hotel with Aunt Nancy," Leigh said.

"She threw up all over and had her head in the toilet when we left," Scott added.

Dakota looked at Dawn. "Is she going to be all right?" he asked.

"She'll be fine, just her nerves, that's all. She sends you her love and says she'll see you next time," Dawn answered him.

Pulling something out of her pocket and putting it in Dakota's hand Lou said, "Daddy Dakota, look what I colored you." As he opened it, he smiled. "Now that's really pretty. Did you do this all by yourself?"

"Yep, except Leigh helped me with the face," she said so proudly. "But Scott drew it for me to color. He's an artist like you, Daddy."

"Yes, he is. In fact, I've even used some of his drawings for my wood burning." Dakota smiled at Scott. Smiling at what Dakota had said, Scott stood straight and proud. Leigh and Scott then returned to their seats, but Lou was not about to give up sitting on Dakota's lap. She snuggled right into him. Dakota could see this was going to be Daddy's little girl.

Dakota had on a short sleeve shirt and the children noticed the tattoos on his arms. They were done in blue ink and weren't colored in.

"Why did you draw on yourself, Daddy Dakota?" Lou asked. "Mom says we should never take an ink pen and do that. We could get poison in our blood."

"Silly, that's not an ink pen. Guys have those and they're called tattoos," Leigh said.

"That's right, there's a special way we do it and it will never wash off. It's done with a needle, sort of like getting a lot of shots," Dakota told her.

"I don't think I'd like that. I don't like shots," Lou said.

"That's cause you're a girl, guys are tougher," Scott said.

"Maybe," Leigh said to Scott, "But girls are smarter."

Dakota could see where this was leading and changed the subject. "You see that counter over there? Well I'll bet you'd all love an ice-cream cone. Take this money over to that man in the white hat. Tell him you're my kids and he'll give you an extra scoop. The ice cream here is homemade. You won't find better ice-cream in all of Louisiana." The children took the money and walked over to the counter.

"Dakota, are you sure that's safe?" Dawn asked with concern.

"Honey, trust me. There's not one person in this room that would dare harm a hair on any of their heads. Relax Mom, they'll be fine." Looking over his shoulder at them, and then looking back at Dawn he said, "They sure are some cuties."

"Thank you, but believe me they can be a handful."

"What kid can't be at times? All they need is just a little love and understanding. I can tell by their letters and the phone calls that you do a great job with them."

"I really try, but sometimes I wonder if I'm doing it all ok."

"Don't worry Mom, you're doing great, they love and

respect you. Not creating respect for parents is where most people now days go wrong. A lot of children are free to run and no one cares. The most important thing a child wants from their parent is love, not what they can buy them or do for them. You give them both love and your time," he said.

Dawn couldn't believe how much Dakota knew about children. He'd never been married or had any of his own. *"What a great father he would be,"* she thought.

"Someday, this will all be over and we'll be together. Then you won't have to be on your own with them, but until then, I'll do the best I can from here."

"Dakota, you wouldn't believe how much you help now. I've seen the change in them since you've come into our lives. Just knowing they can talk to you about anything they want without you thinking they're silly, makes a big difference. I know Leigh writes to you all the time. She really enjoys the fact that you don't tell me what she writes. Having someone other than Mom she can confide in makes all the difference in the world," Dawn said with love in her voice.

"Children need adults to understand their problems. They may not seem big to us, but to them they're important. If more adults would take time with children, maybe this prison and other prisons wouldn't be so full. I'm not saying that's the only reason that people are in prison, but I do know that if more parents would spend time with their children, then the children wouldn't have to do bad things to get attention. When a child grows up with only getting attention when they're bad, then that teaches them it's a way of life. Then when adults they do the same thing. Guess you could say they were conditioned to be that way," Dakota said seriously.

As Dawn looked around the room, she turned to Dakota and said, "I never thought about it that way."

"After all these years in here, you learn a lot about these inmates, and the kind of life they had before. We have guys in here from all walks of life, rich, poor and middle class. Now

I'm not saying, that every inmate in here had a bad childhood and that you should feel sorry for them. We all have choices, Dawn. It's what we do with these choices that make us what we are today and in the future."

When the children came back with their ice cream cones, each one of them had a different flavor. They were all smiles and thanked Dakota for the ice cream.

"You know we have our own dairy farm here. Inmates work there. Then other inmates work in the factory where the ice cream is made. We also have a factory where we can our own food."

"Really, you have cows here?" Lou asked.

"Yep, cows, pigs and lots of crops," Dakota answered her.

"Do you get to work with the cows and pigs?" Lou asked.

"No, honey I work with the dogs and the police. The other inmates work on the farms."

"Do you ever have puppies?" Leigh asked.

"Yes, we have puppies all the time. We raise them and then they go to a nice police officer to be his dog," Dakota said.

"That's neat. How many dogs do you have?" Scott asked.

"Oh, about thirty, I'd say. We have different breeds for different things," Dakota told him. "Like for tracking when someone is lost. Or maybe a drug dog will find drugs someone is hiding. Things like that," Dakota said.

"That's cool. I want to be a police officer when I grow up," Leigh told him.

"Really? Well I think that's great," Dakota told Leigh.

As the children visited with Dakota, Dawn was thinking to herself and wishing they could take this man home with them. It was going to be hard to leave him there. She was wondering when they would see each other again. She loved him so much and to go months and years without seeing him would just tear her apart.

Sensing something was heavy on her mind, Dakota reached over and took her hand in his. She looked up at him. He could see in her eyes a sadness that he didn't want there, but knew it couldn't be helped. He gave her hand a little squeeze and smiled at her. She smiled back.

"Now that's better," he said. "Things will be just fine. You just think happy thoughts and they will come true."

"If that's all it takes, I'll think happy thoughts twenty-four hours a day, and just maybe I'll put in a few thoughts of you," Dawn said.

"Just a few?" Dakota teased.

"Mom says we might come back and see you in July," Lou said.

"Did she now?" Dakota said looking at Dawn.

"Yep, she said that maybe a couple times a year we could until you came home," Scott added.

"Mom says she's thinking about moving to Kentucky so that maybe we could see you even more than that, if she can find a place and a job. Aunt Nancy said she'd help," Leigh put in.

Dakota looked at Dawn. "That's kinda a big move, don't you think?" he said.

"Well it has crossed my mind. I just thought it would put us in the middle. You know only ten hours from home and about ten hours from you. This way we could see you at least twice a month," Dawn said.

"I think we should talk about this, don't you?" he said.

"Yes, wouldn't it be great Dakota if the children and I were closer? Than we could see you more often," Dawn said.

"Honey, there's nothing more that I would like than seeing you and the children, well except maybe one, living with ya'll would be better," Dakota said.

"Daddy Dakota, Mom says you used to hunt deer, why would you want to kill Bambi?" Lou said.

Dakota looked at Dawn for help on this, seeing he was on his own as Dawn just smiled back. He answered, "Well Darling, I would never kill Bambi. When a man, or even a woman goes hunting, they don't kill baby deer. We hunt the big ones. It's like the beef or pork your ma buys in the store. If there are too many deer and no one hunts them, then there won't be enough food for them in the winter. So if we thin down the population some, the rest can survive." Dakota really hoped she would understand this.

"Oh so you kill the really old ones?" Lou asked. Hoping this was his out, Dakota answered. "Yes, just the old ones and we let the young ones go."

"Do you have a coon skin hat, you know like Davy Crocket?" Lou asked.

"Why would you ask him that?" Dawn wanted to know.

"'Cause, Davy Crocket had one and he was a hunter, and Daniel Boon had one too," Lou said.

"No, I don't have a coon skin hat, but ya know, maybe I should get one. You're right, all the great hunters have one," Dakota said as he tickled her.

Lou started laughing and gave Dakota a big hug. "Daddy Dakota, when you get home will you get me a coon hat too?"

"You can count on it, and maybe we'll get your ma to make you some boots made out of a deer hide," Dakota added.

"Really now, what makes you think I'm going to do that?" Dawn asked.

"Well you did say you were part Indian, didn't you? You know squaws chew the fat off of the hide, and make clothes and such out of it," Dakota said with a laugh.

"Yuck, I wouldn't do that," Leigh said.

"He's just joking, the Indian women didn't really do that," Dawn said. "They use to stake out the hides, stretch them and scrape the fat off with a knife and rocks."

"Dakota may be part Indian himself children, and therefore, like the Indians he tells a good story," Dawn said.

"I'll have you know Ma'am, I am part Indian. I used to be pretty darn good with my bow and arrow, a wooden arrow at that," Dakota said proudly.

"Just like the old arrows the Indians use to use in the

cowboy days?" Scott asked.

"The very same kind. I'll show you kids when I get home how to use one." Dakota smiled.

Dakota told the children stories about Crystal Valley, where he grew up. He told them about the horses he use to have and how he painted himself up as a warrior one time to go out on a hunt. He told them about the times he went to the woods to chop down trees for the winter wood heat, about the garden they use to have, and how his ma would can all the things from the garden. Dakota really had them laughing when he told them the story about his brother getting sprayed by the skunk.

After about an hour more, the children were getting restless. Dakota sensed they needed to stretch their legs. "Are you kids ready for another ice cream cone?" Dakota asked.

"Can we go get another ice cream Mom?" Leigh asked.

"Yes, you may," Dawn said.

With the children gone, Dakota squeezed Dawn's hand lightly. "Honey, I know you want to see me more and Darling I want to see you too, but not like this. I want to be home with you and the children. If you're thinking of moving because you really want to, then that's fine. If you're thinking about moving to be closer to me, just so you can see me more, than Honey, please stay in Michigan." Seeing this caused a hurt look on her face, he continued, "It's not that I don't want to see you, Darling, because I do, but I'll be honest with you. I'm not as tough as you think I am. Honey, watching you walk out those doors and knowing I can't go with you tears me up, more than I can tell you. Having you only a few hours away, being so close and yet so far out of reach would drive me crazy. I know it's hard for you to understand, but I need to keep my head straight to work on getting out of here. I love you Dawn and I want to be with you, not just for a few hours here and there, but to be with you daily. I know a few people and I've been trying really hard to get a hearing with the parole board. If the parole board approves it, then I'd be out on parole and home with you and the children."

Sadly Dawn said, "I know how you feel about wanting to be together. I want that too, Dakota. What I don't understand is why did you want us to come and visit you now? The last thing I want to do is tear you up. I never even thought about it that way. I thought it would make you happy to see us."

Seeing her sadness was tearing him up. He took his other hand and gently stroked the side of her face, "Darling, seeing you and those children does make me happy, more than I can tell you, but watching you go will tear me up inside. We needed to see each other Dawn, and in doing so, we will both be happy and hurt by it. Sometimes, Darling, love hurts, and this is one of those times, but it won't be forever. We'll be together someday. Honey, I know it's hard for you to understand, but please be patient and give me the time I need to get out of here. When I come home, I'll show you more love and happiness then you have ever known. Until then Dawn, know that wherever you go, or wherever you are, that my love goes with you. What we have between us is real and only comes once in a lifetime."

Dawn didn't know what to say to this. He was right. How could she know what it would be like to have someone visit you in prison, then walk away, and go back to their life, leaving you behind. She tried to see his point of view, but oh how she loved him and wanted to be near him. Her feelings were all mixed up. Would this be the last time she'd see him? It could take months or even years for him to get on parole, what would she do until then? Her eyes started to fill with tears, but she knew she couldn't let them go. As she looked at him, Dakota knew this was tearing her up.

"Damn, I didn't want to do this to her," he thought. *"But we really needed to see each other."* As he held her hand he leaned over and kissed her and said, "I love you, and it's going to be all right."

"I love you, and I do believe you that it will be all right and

142

we will be together someday. But Dakota, I will miss you dearly until that day comes. Just promise me one thing," she pleaded.

"If I can Honey, what is it?"

"That this won't be the only time we can see you. I can't live with that thought Dakota. To go on for months or years with never seeing you until you're free, is more than I can take. I know I'm being selfish, but you always told me to be honest. I'd rather hurt seeing you like this, than not see you at all," she said as a tear slipped down her cheek.

"Honey, when the time comes, we'll both decide when the next visit will be. Ok?"

"Ok, I can live with that," Dawn said.

"You drive a hard bargain, Mrs. Deer. Must be that bull in you, you know the Taurus?"

Dawn smiled, "Yes, and you poor man, we have two more in the family besides me. How will you ever handle us?"

He gently kissed her. "With tender love and lots of it."

"Mom, look at this. That man gave us three scoops this time! Said it was because we were Dakota's kids." Lou beamed.

"That was really nice of him. Did you thank him for it?" Dawn said.

"Yes Ma'am, we all did. He asked us if we were going to get our pictures taken today," Scott said.

"Daddy Dakota, does that mean they want to take our mug shot, like on T.V.?" Lou asked.

"No, Lou, it means, there's an inmate here who takes pictures of the men and their family," Dakota said.

"Well I think that's a great idea," Leigh said. "After we're done with our ice cream, let's have a family picture done."

"That sounds good to me," Dawn smiled.

"I'd really like that too," Dakota said.

When the children were done with their ice cream, they all walked over to where the man was taking pictures. He took several family pictures, and then Leigh wanted to know if Dakota and Dawn were going to have their picture taken as a couple. When the pictures were done and the inmate was paid, they walked back to their table. As they looked over the pictures, a voice over the loud speaker said, "Inmate Deer please report."

"I'll be right back," Dakota said.

"Mom, where's Daddy Dakota going?" Lou asked.

"Oh, he's just checking in, I'm sure," Dawn answered her. Dawn's heart was sinking, as she looked at her watch. *"It's been four hours,"* she thought to herself. She knew the visit with Dakota was over.

As Dakota walked back to them, the look on his face said it all. Dawn's throat tightened.

"It's time for me to go back," Dakota said to Dawn. As he bent down on one knee to be at face level with the smallest child, he said to them, "Now I want you all to be good for your ma, and keep doing good in school. Ya know your ma sends me your report cards. I'm really proud of all you kids. I'll write, and you be sure to write me back. I'll call you in a few days to see how your trip was home."

Lou put her arms around Dakota's neck, "I love you Daddy Dakota."

"I love you too," he told her.

Leigh walked up to Dakota with tears in her eyes, "Daddy Dakota, can't you come home with us now? They know you're not a bad man. We need you more than they do." Dakota looked up at Dawn, then back at Leigh. He hugged her and said. "Honey, when my job is done here, I'll be home, I promise. Until then, you just be a good girl and I'll be thinking about you."

He hugged her and said he loved her. Then Dakota looked at Scott. "Well young man, it seems it'll be up to you to take care of your ma and sisters until I get home. I'm counting on you to be the man of the house. Can you do that for me?"

"Yes Sir," Scott said choked up.

"I'm proud of you, Son. Come over here and give me a hug," Dakota said. Scott gave Dakota a hug and said to him, "I love you Dad."

"I love you, Son," Dakota said.

Dakota then stood up and looked at Dawn. Taking her hand he said, "Come on, I'll walk you to the front desk." As they walked up to the front desk, Dakota said to Dawn, "Honey, I know it will be hard to walk out, but it's not the last time you'll see me. Keep that in mind and it'll help."

Up at the front desk, Dakota, gave the children one last hug, then took Dawn in his arms. "Mrs. Deer, remember one thing. I love you and will always love you." Then he bent and kissed her softly on the lips, when Dawn responded with her heart, Dakota deepened the kiss.

"Mom, are you two coming up for air?" Leigh asked.

Dakota ended the kiss and winked at Leigh. Looking back at Dawn, he saw the tears in her eyes. Taking his fingers and wiping the tears dry, he whispered in her ear, "It'll be all right. I'll be home soon."

"I love you, Dakota," Dawn said through her tears.

Then she turned and with the children walked towards the guard waiting to let them out. As they followed Helen back to the bus Helen said to Leigh, "Dakota's, your Daddy?"

"Yes Ma'am, and I just want him to come home," Leigh said.

"He'll be home. Honey, you just wait and see," Helen said.

When Dawn and the children returned to the hotel, Nancy and the other children were out in the pool. "Hey, how did your visit go?" Nancy asked.

"It was great." Then turning to Lynn, Leigh said, "You should have seen all the inmates. The bus ride was cool. We were locked up just like prisoners."

"Daddy Dakota said to tell you he loved you and would see you next time. He hopes you're feeling better," Lou added.

"You should see my dad's arms. He must be the strongest guy in the prison," Scott said proudly.

"So, how are you?" Nancy asked Dawn.

"I'll be all right. I just wish he could have come home with us," Dawn answered.

"He will, just have faith," Nancy said.

Chapter 18

Two months later in Washington, D.C., Dakota was in a meeting with the President. The President was explaining to Dakota that he needed him to go to Europe to handle some foreign security for him.

"You'll be gone about two weeks. I need top security put into place for our diplomats. The embassy has been threatened. If the threats are carried out it could cause a major war."

"When do I leave?" Dakota asked.

"Tonight, I've got a DC9 on stand-by waiting for you. You can go over to the CIA headquarters and pick up whatever you need. I'm sending our best agents with you."

Standing up and shaking the President's hand Dakota said, "I won't let you down, Mr. President, I'll see you in a couple of weeks."

"Thank You, Agent Deer, I knew I could count on you."

Later that evening before Dakota left Washington, D.C. he called Dawn. "Good Evening," Dakota said as Dawn answered the phone.

"I was just thinking about you, Dakota."

"Really now, and what thoughts were those?"

"Oh I was sitting here thinking to myself, I sure wish Dakota would call. Guess I just needed to hear your voice," she said happily.

"So tell me, my darling wife, how are those children of ours doing? Are they being good and helping Mom around the house?"

"Yes Dad, they surely are. I couldn't ask for them to be better. Oh they have their spats over the Nintendo, but that's about it. Yesterday, the kids were out riding their bikes on the bike trail. I guess Scott was following Leigh and he got too close to her bike. Anyway, his tire rubbed hers and caused her to fall down. She ended up cracking the two smallest bones in the back of her right hand, just behind the two small fingers. Kinda messes up her playing her flute in the band for a while."

"Bet Scott feels bad about that. What did the doctors do for her hand?"

"They put a brace on it to keep her from bending her hand. They don't want her to break the bones all the way. It could cause problems if she did. She seems to be doing pretty good though. It hasn't stopped her from riding her bike or roller skating on the bike trail." Dawn laughed.

"It surely amazes me how children bounce back so quickly. I'm glad she's going to be all right."

"They're all out on the bike trail right now. So, Mr. Deer what are you up to lately?"

Dakota didn't really want to lie to Dawn, but he had to come up with some excuse, "Well that's one of the reasons I called. I'm going to be pretty busy down here for the next couple of weeks. We're getting ready for an arts and crafts show. I'm going to be spending all of my free time in my hobby shop. I'll be working until early in the morning. You know that's the only way I make my money. I didn't want you to worry if you don't hear from me. Honey, I'm not really going to have any time to call you."

"Oh," Dawn said, a little let down. "I understand, Dakota."

"When this busy time is over, I'll be calling and writing again. You know I love you, Dawn."

Dawn was sad that she wouldn't hear from Dakota, but she did understand, "Yes, Dakota, I know that. It's just that I'll miss you. You've spoiled me with letters almost daily and the phone calls I really look forward to, but Honey I do understand. Just don't forget about me."

"Darling, to forget about you and the children would be like not breathing. Maybe you should keep writing to me. You know just to make sure I don't forget you," Dakota teased her.

"Keep talking like that and I'm sure I could come up with

a few letters to nag you with. That way I could sound like a real wife," Dawn said trying to sound firm.

Dakota laughed at that, "And what makes you think you don't already sound like a real wife? After all, you are my wife, Mrs. Deer, and it couldn't get any more real than that."

When they had talked over an hour Dakota said, "Well Honey, I really think we should get off the phone. I love you and I'll be calling in a few weeks. You take care of those children and tell them I love them."

"I'll miss you Dakota, and I love you too."

Chapter 19

On the flight over to Europe, Dakota and the other agents went over the plans for the embassy. As they looked over the blueprints of the embassy, Dakota marked each spot that had a weakness in security. "We will improve these spots gentlemen, and the grounds around the embassy will have heightened security. We shall install the new security system and put it to the test. The mail will even go through a security check before it's delivered to the ambassadors. Anything that comes into the embassy will be checked."

The first week was spent installing the new security system while leaving the old one active. Dakota and the other agents worked all night long while the embassy was quiet. Each agent was a specialist in his field.

The following week the security system was tested. On the fourth night of testing Dakota received a phone call from one of the agents in Michigan.

"Agent Deer?"

"This is Agent Deer"

"Agent Deer, this is Agent Jones, we have a problem here in Michigan, Sir."

Knowing this had to do with Dawn and the children, Dakota answered him, "And what kind of a problem is that?"

Glad of the miles between them Agent Jones reluctantly replied, "It's the boy Sir, he's well he's sort of disappeared. We think maybe he's been kidnapped."

"He's sort of disappeared? And you think maybe he's been kidnapped?" Now losing his temper Dakota added, "What the hell's going on back there?"

The agents in the security office at the embassy turned and looked at Dakota. No one spoke a word. When Agent Deer got fired up, heads would roll, and they all knew someone in the states was in deep trouble.

"Well Sir, the children were all out riding their bikes on the bike trail. Scott is always the last one back. When he didn't show up, we went looking for him. We found his bike by the edge of the woods. We searched the woods and found no sign of him anywhere. We had the tracking dog look for him, but he lost the trail by the gas station a mile south from where we found the bike. We feel someone took him by car from the gas station," Agent Jones told him.

Steaming mad, Dakota said, "Where are the other children?"

"They are with their mother at the house. She's called the police and they are on their way to her house. One of our agents, Agent Potter, will be with the police, as a policeman, to find out more from her."

Dakota felt better knowing Chew would be there. After all the years they had spent working at the prison together, Dakota knew he could count on Chew.

"You listen to me, Agent Jones. If one hair on that boy's head is even out of place when he's found, you'll have me to deal with...and Agent Jones?"

"Yes Sir, Agent Deer?"

"That lady and children you've been watching!" Dakota said firmly.

"Yes Sir?"

Dakota's temper really flamed up, "I have a personal interest in them. That happens to be MY WIFE AND CHILDREN. Now you might start looking in the direction of a Tom Brown from Detroit. He would have reason to kidnap my son. His files are on record at the CIA. I'm leaving tonight to fly back to Michigan and you'd better have my son back with his mother by the time I get there. Do I make myself clear? Agent Jones, my wife has no idea I'm an agent. She thinks I'm in prison down south. Now get on this!"

"Oh Shit! I mean, Yes Sir, Agent Deer."

As Dakota hung up the phone he turned and looked at the

agents in the office. No one said a word, but everyone had their mouths open in shock. In all the years they had known Agent Deer, not one of them knew he had a wife.

"The testing seems to be going well, and we've had no problems with it. As it stands right now, a mouse couldn't get pass the security we've put into place. Keep testing it and if you have any problems give me a call. As you have all heard, I'm leaving tonight to fly back to Michigan. I'll be in touch. Are there any questions?" Dakota asked them.

At first no one said anything, then one Agent spoke up. "Agent Deer, I know I speak for all of us, we hope your boy will be all right." The rest of the agents nodded their heads in agreement.

"Thank you," Dakota said and then he left the room.

On his flight back to the states, Dakota knew he shouldn't call Dawn. After all he had told her he would be busy for a few weeks. Worrying about her and the children got the best of him. He picked up the phone and called. Trying to sound normal he said, "Hello Darling."

"Dakota, it's just awful. Something has happened to Scott. He's missing, Dakota! The police are looking for him and they think he's been kidnapped. Dakota, I'm really scared," Dawn said as she broke into tears.

"What happened Dawn? Come on, Darling, talk to me."

"He was out riding his bike and never came home. The girls and I looked for him, Dakota, and all we found was his bike. I called the police and they're looking for him now. Dakota, I think Tom's got him."

Even though Dakota thought the same thing, he asked Dawn, "What makes you think Tom's got him Dawn?"

"When the judge ordered that Tom never see the children again at our divorce, Tom called me a few days later. He said that it wasn't over and that someday he would have his son back, even if it meant him taking him out of the country. I didn't believe him. I thought he was just angry and trying to upset me. Dakota, that was over two years ago. The children haven't even received a birthday card, a phone call, or anything from him in the past two years."

"Did you tell the police this?"

"Yes, but they feel since Tom has had no contact with the children or me in the past two years, that it's not likely to be him. They feel that a stranger might have taken Scott."

"Have you tried calling Tom?"

"Yes, I called his house and got no answer. Then I called his work and they told me that he no longer works there."

Dakota's stomach turned at hearing that, "Did they say how long ago that he quit?"

"I asked that and they said about two weeks ago. Maybe the police are right, Dakota. Maybe it's not Tom."

"No," Dakota thought to himself, *"it's Tom all right. He quit his job went up north and watched the children for a couple weeks before he made his move."*

"Dawn, has Tom ever mentioned to you about going to another country? You know for vacation or whatever?"

"Well he did mention going to Canada someday on vacation, but Dakota that was years ago," Dawn said sounding confused.

"Did he ever say what part of Canada?"

"Yes, he thought we should take the children camping in Quebec. Something about a Lake Pigon."

"Did you ever go there?"

"No, I thought the children were too small at the time. Back then we would've had to have I.D. for them to get back into the U.S. I know I was silly, but I was afraid that the Canadian government would keep my children."

"That's my girl, always watching out for her babies," Dakota thought. "Dawn, if Tom's got him you know you don't have to worry. Tom won't harm him, keep that in mind."

"I have thought about that, Dakota, Tom would never hurt the children, just me. Dakota, now would be a good time to use your connection with God to bring my son home," she said desperately.

"Honey, I have a few connections with people down here. Let me make a few phone calls and see what I can do. I'll call you back in a few hours."

"I love you Dakota, I really wish you were here."

"Honey, I'm closer at times than you think," Dakota thought to himself. "Now let me go and I'll call you later. Scott's going to be all right."

Dakota got up from his seat and walked to the front of the plane. He opened the door to the cockpit and asked the pilot if they had an atlas he could borrow. They gave him one; he walked back to his seat and put the atlas on the table. As he looked at the Quebec area he looked around the map for a Lake Pigon. Finding none, he looked at the Ontario area there he found a Lake Nipigon.

"That's got to be it," Dakota said to himself. Reaching for the phone Dakota dialed a number.

"CIA Agent Ward speaking."

"Agent Ward, this is Agent Deer. Patch me through to Colonel Williams."

"Yes Sir," Agent Ward said. Dakota could hear the call being transferred.

"Hello, Colonel Williams speaking."

"Colonel Williams, it's Agent Deer."

"Agent Deer, what can I do for you?"

"I need a team of men sent to Lake Nipigon, in Ontario, Canada. I'm sending you a fax, with a picture of a boy that has been kidnapped. I want this boy recovered, unharmed."

"Who is this boy Agent Deer?" Colonel Williams asked.

"My son, Colonel Williams. I'm on my way back from Europe now and will meet the team one mile south of a town called Marathon. Tell them this is a code red operation. I want the best sharp shooters we've got."

"You've got it, Agent Deer. They'll be on their way within

the hour. Good luck Agent Deer, I hope your son will be all right."

"Thank you, Colonel Williams. Agent Deer out."

Dakota walked to the front of the plane, "There's been a change of plans, we're not going to Michigan after all. I need you to take me to Ontario, Canada, as close as you can get me to a town called Marathon."

"Will do, Agent Deer. It'll be about ten hours before we're there, Sir," the pilot replied

Dakota nodded to the pilot and walked back to his seat.

When Dakota was seated he wondered if Tom would really harm Scott in any way. *"The man's sick,"* he thought. Dakota picked up the phone and dialed again.

"Agent Jones," Agent Jones answered.

"Agent Deer here. So Agent Jones, what have you found out?"

"Well Sir, we found out that Tom Brown quit his job two weeks ago. We checked out his address and went into his house. It appears he's packed a few things, clothes, shaving gear, but nothing big. It appears he's gone on vacation."

"And do we know where he went, Agent Jones?"

"We checked with his neighbors and none of them seem to really know the guy. They say he's quiet and keeps to himself. Most of them don't even know his name. Agent Potter has issued an A.P.B. on his car. His picture has been distributed to the local and state police. They know there is a kidnapping involved."

"I want you and the other agents to keep an eye on the house, and my family. Agent Jones, don't let anything else happen. I'll be seeing you soon."

"Yes Sir, Agent Deer," Agent Jones said and hung up the phone.

Something about this just didn't make sense; Dawn's words came back to Dakota. "Tom would never hurt the children, just me." Why did this bother him so much? The ringing of

Dakota's phone brought him out of his thought.

"Agent Deer here," Dakota said.

"Dakota, it's Chew."

"Chew, you can't know how glad I am that you're there. Look, I'm on my way to Canada. I think Tom's taken Scott there. But for some reason Chew, I don't know call it a hunch, I think Tom's going to go after Dawn and the girls."

"What makes you think that?"

"It's something Dawn said. She told me Tom would never hurt the children, just her."

"What do you want me to do Dakota?" Chew asked.

"Stay with her Chew, give her some line about police protection. In case the kidnaper calls for a ransom, set up a trace on her phone. Hell I don't know Chew, think of something."

Chew could hear the frustration in Dakota's voice. He knew Dakota was losing his objectiveness on this situation.

"Dakota, you're too close. Back off and think like an agent. You're not going to do anyone any good if you keep thinking like a husband and father. Now get your act together man and do it now! I've already got someone at the house and a tracer is already in place. I plan on staying there tonight."

"Good, thanks Chew."

"I've read the CIA files on this guy and he's a Lou Lou. If he even tries to get close to Dawn and the girls, I'm taking him out," Chew said firmly.

"No, Chew, just take him down. I don't want the girls or Dawn to see that. Let the inmates in prison have him."

"It's your call Dakota. Agent Potter out."

"It's now been over twenty-four hours since Scott disappeared. Tom could have Scott anywhere by now," Dakota thought as he paced back and forth on the plane. *"What if I'm wrong and he doesn't take him to Lake Nipigon?"*

Back in Montague, Agent Chew Potter was meeting with the other agents. "We have new information on Tom Brown. It seems his car was spotted at the gas station about the time Scott was kidnapped. However, no one saw the boy with him. The gas station attendant identified Mr. Brown when he was shown his picture. He says Tom Brown filled up his car, bought lunchmeat, bread, chips, pop and a few sports drinks. He paid for them by credit card. He said that Tom Brown seemed in a hurry and was a strange man. He's driving a black Ford Mustang with the plates TYG123. Gentlemen, my thoughts are this, what if our Mr. Brown isn't working alone? The gas station was busy that day and my thoughts are even if he had Scott gagged and tied; he could have still made some sort of noise. Since no one heard a thing, that leads me to believe that maybe he has an accomplice working with him, and at some point they'll meet up."

"Do we have any idea of who this person could be?" asked Agent Jones.

"That's what I plan on finding out tonight. I'll be staying with Mrs. Deer and the children, for police protection, and I'll talk to her. She may be able to fill me in on a few of Tom's friends. I'm waiting for the lab results on the fingerprints taken from the boy's bike. Hopefully we'll find something there," Agent Potter said.

Chapter 20

The cabin was just ahead. She could see it. It was nestled right where Tom said it would be.

"Are we almost there, Aunt Liz?" Scott asked.

"Yes, honey we are. See that cabin right there? That's where we are going," Liz answered.

"Mom and the girls will really like this. It's a good idea, us getting here first and cleaning it all up for them," Scott said smiling.

As she parked the car she took her hand and placed it on Scott's head and tousled his hair. "I'm sure they will. Now let's get unpacked and have some fun."

They unpacked the car and carried everything into the cabin. "Wow, would you look at this!" Scott said. "Look at it all, Aunt Liz." Scott was pointing to the large T.V., a Nintendo game player, a tower filled with Nintendo games and videos for the VCR, the cordless remote car, new clothes, and tons of more things he was sure would catch his sister's interest once they got here.

Liz could see that Tom went way overboard this time, but it couldn't hurt. After all, look at the pleased look on Scott's face. "So what do you think?"

"Whose is all this?" Scott asked.

"It's yours and your sisters'. It's a surprise," Liz said.

Once they explored the cabin, Liz said to Scott, "I've never been here myself, but I was told that out back there's a shed. Let's go look and see what's in there."

"This is great. Sure let's go. I'll find the shed first. After all the man of the house needs to watch for bears and such in the woods," Scott said.

"Or be the first to the loot, right Scott?" Liz teased him.

"Yes Ma'am, it's a hard job, being the first one to find all

158

the surprises."

About thirty yards from the back porch stood a wooden shed, as Scott and Liz opened the door, Scott's mouth dropped. "Aunt Liz, I don't understand what's going on. There are new bikes and skate boards in here."

"Don't you like all this? Your mom, dad and I worked so hard to make it nice for you and the girls."

"What do you mean, my dad?" Scott asked.

"Come on let's go sit on the back porch and I'll explain it all to you," Liz said. As they walked up to the cabin they took in the view. As they sat down on the porch Liz started to explain. "You see, since your mom and dad's divorce, Tom hasn't been allowed to visit you kids, but that doesn't mean he didn't still love you all very much. Anyway, your mom still lets him know how you all are doing in school. She sends him pictures of you all and so on. Well, your dad thought that your mom and you kids could use a break. So he told your mom he'd pay for the cabin for a week if she'd take you kids on the trip. She said yes. Since he can't be here himself while you're all having a good time, he thought he'd fill it full of gifts for you and your sisters. Your mom told me she was pretty sure that your dad would spoil you kids with gifts here, but that you all needed the break, so she didn't mind."

Scott sat on the porch and looked around the cabin. *"It must be the way Aunt Liz was telling it, after all there was no sing of Tom anywhere. Mom had said she wanted to go camping someday again. This would be much better than that pop-up they lived in for a while,"* he thought. "Well Aunt Liz, do you think we should take in some fire wood for the fire place in the living room? I know my mom would enjoy watching a fire in that. This is the kind of log cabin my mom has always talked about. I know she's going to like it here," Scott said.

Smiling at Scott and putting her hand out to him, Liz thought to herself, *"Tom was right Scott did buy that story. There was no threat to his mom. And this was something his mom had always wanted, to stay in a nice log cabin."* "I do believe you're right. Your mom is going to love it here. I can't wait for your mom and sisters to join us," Liz said.

Liz and Scott gathered wood for the fireplace and took it into the cabin. Scott worked on building the fire as Liz looked out the big picture window. She let her mind wander to the plans that she and Tom had made.

"You know, Liz, with Dawn out of the way, we'll be one big happy family. Within a month of Dawn's death, we'll be married. The children love you and think the world of you. It won't take them long and they'll look on you as their mother," Tom told Liz.

"Tom, you know I love you and the children. Nothing could make me happier than to be a family," Liz said.

"I'll meet you at the cabin. I love you, Liz."

"I love you too," Liz said as they kissed.

"Yes, little Miss Dawn was going to get hers. If Dawn thought for even one moment that Liz would forgive her for stealing Dakota's heart she had another thing coming," Liz thought back to the time that Dawn had shared her news with her childhood friend.

"Oh Liz, isn't it great, Dakota's in love with me," Dawn said.

"And to think Dawn, you're the one who thought years ago that I was crazy to be involved with a man in prison," Liz teased her.

"I know, but we were just kids, right out of high school. What did we know then of real love?" Dawn said.

"You're right, that was a long time ago, but Dakota will always have a special place in my heart, you know he was my first love, and you know what they say about first loves," Liz said with a tone Dawn wasn't sure how to take.

Scott's voice brought Liz out of her daydream. "Aunt Liz, what do you think of my fire?"

Liz turned to look back at Scott and the fireplace. "Oh,

that's great! Your mom will just love it."

Chapter 21

Dakota paced back and forth on the plane. He couldn't take it any longer. He walked into the cockpit. "How much longer before we're there?"

"About four hours, Sir," the pilot answered.

"Damn!" Dakota said looking at his watch.

"Sir, I'm pushing her as fast as she'll go," the pilot said.

"Thanks," Dakota said and walked out of the cockpit. He walked back to his seat and picked up the phone, then put it back down. Feeling helpless and wanting to be in two different places at the same time, Dakota knew he was losing his edge. He wanted to be with Dawn and comfort her and at the same time he wanted to be in Canada to protect Scott.

Picking up the phone Dakota called Dawn. "Hello," Dawn said.

"God she sounds stressed out," he thought. "Hello Darling, it's me. How ya doing?"

"Not too good. Dakota, I can't handle this," Dawn said broken up.

"Yes you can. Scott needs you to keep yourself together. So tell me Darling, what's the update?"

"A police officer named Captain Potter is here with us. He's really a nice man. The police have a tracer on the phone in case Tom calls. Captain Potter says there are men watching the house in case Tom or someone tries to approach us. They are telling us to act as normal as we can. Tell me, Dakota, how do we do that?" Dawn said, pleading.

When Dakota heard Dawn's voice, he wanted to jump through the phone and just hold her. "I promise you, Dawn, everything will be all right. Just do as Captain Potter tells you to do. If it seems strange, do it anyway, Darling, he knows what he's doing."

"How do you know, Dakota you don't even know him?"

"Trust me, Honey, these men are trained for this type of thing. How are the girls holding up?"

"They're sitting around in the living room, just waiting. Dakota they feel it's their fault for leaving Scott behind."

"Honey, it's not their fault, they were being kids. It's Tom's fault! We'll get Scott back!" Dakota said a little shorter then he planed.

"Dakota?"

"Look, I'm sorry for sounding so short. It's just that I wish I could be there with you and the girls. Being down here and not being able to help you, just frustrates me. Look, I'm going to let you go, I don't want to tie the line up any longer in case Tom tries to call."

"O.K. I love you, Dakota."

"I love ya'll too. I'll call again in a while."

Captain Potter was looking out the window while Dawn was on the phone with Dakota. *"Damn,"* he thought to himself, *"Dakota must be a basket case. Being personally involved wasn't a good thing. He wouldn't stay objective, but then all the training in the world couldn't teach you how to handle this."*

As Dawn hung up the phone Captain Potter turned to her, "Are you all right Ma'am?"

"Yes, thank you. That was Dakota, he's my…he's my…he's the man I love, but he lives out of state."

"Yes Ma'am," Captain Potter said. Damn this lady was sweet. No wonder Dakota fell in love with her. "Ma'am, if there's anything I can do for you, please don't hesitate to ask."

A couple of hours went by and the phone rang. Dawn looked at Captain Potter, he nodded his head, and Dawn picked up the phone.

"Hello," she said with caution to her voice.

"Dawn, I'm not going to pusy-foot around with you, so I'll get straight to the point. I know the cops are there and most

163

likely they have the phone tapped. I want you and the girls to get into your car and meet me where we went on our first date. Alone. If you tell the cops or if they follow you, you'll never see Scott alive again. I have nothing to lose here Dawn. Do you understand?" Tom said.

"Yes Tom, let me talk to Scott," Dawn pleaded.

"He's not here. If something happens to me, no one will ever find him. Now get going!"

"Tom wait," Dawn said, but Tom had already hung up.

Captain Potter looked at the officer with the tracing machine; he shook his head at Captain Potter. "Damn, he wasn't on the phone long enough," Captain Potter said.

As they listened to the tape of the phone conversation Chew knew, he didn't like this. "Dawn, you can't go, it's not safe."

Dawn stood firm and looked at Captain Potter, "If I don't go, Captain Potter, I'll never see my son again. You don't know Tom. He'll do what he says. I'm going!"

"Where was your first date?" Captain Potter asked Dawn.

"I can't tell you, and Captain Potter, no one can follow me!" Dawn said firmly.

"Calm down, Dawn, now listen to me," but right then Captain Potter spotted the ring on Dawn's finger, the one that Dakota had made her. He looked at her again and said, "Ok. Dawn no one will follow you. Take no chances and don't piss Tom off. Do whatever he says."

"I will. Come on girls, let's go." With that they walked out the door, got into her car and left.

"All units this is Captain Potter no one is to move. Do not follow Ms. Star, I repeat do not follow Ms. Star."

None of the police units moved. As they watched Dawn drive by they could see the girls in the car with her.

Agent Potter picked up his cell phone and dialed. Dakota answered on the other end. "Agent Deer here."

"Dakota, this is Chew. Look, Tom called. He has Scott. He threatened to kill him if Dawn and the girls didn't meet him where Dawn and Tom had their first date."

"Thank God, we've got a break in this. So where is he? How many units did you send?" Dakota sounded relived.

"I don't know where he's at.... and no, I didn't send units. Tom said if anyone followed her, he'd kill Scott," Chew said.

"What do you mean, you didn't send units? Where's Dawn now?"

"She's gone. She went to meet Tom," Chew answered him.

"Sure, sounds like a grand idea. Send a helpless woman with three young girls to meet a madman." Then raising his voice, Dakota said, "What the hell's the matter with you Chew?"

"Dakota, if you would pull your head out of where the sun doesn't shine, you might remember a certain ring you gave Miss Dawn. I already have the satellite scanning where she is. And unmarked cars with our agents are ready to move. Now Agent Deer, if you would care to discuss the rest of our plans, I would be more than happy to listen," Chew said.

"Damn, Chew, I'm sorry. You're right, I'm not thinking clearly."

"Really? I hadn't noticed. I thought maybe you's just being that half-breed again. Ya know thinking with half of a brain."

Dakota chuckled, "Ok, I deserved that. I'm walking over to the satellite-tracing unit now. Do you have one there?"

"Do Indians eat buffalo?"

"Are you done being a smart-ass?" Dakota asked.

"Doubt it, as I recall this is the way we are through most of our missions. It keeps us thinking straight. Yes, I'm looking at the satellite tracing unit now," Chew said smiling.

"Looks like they are heading north. How long ago did she leave?"

"About fifteen minutes ago," Chew answered.

"If my hunch is right, Tom will end up taking them to Canada. I'll be there and landed before they reach the Mackinaw Bridge. I have a special forces unit meeting me in Canada."

"I'll be following them in one of our unmarked cars...and Dakota?"

"Yea, Chew?"

"Be only an agent. Put that heart of yours back in its steel case...you'll do everyone more good that way. Agent Potter out!"

Dakota took a deep breath, "Agent Deer out."

Chapter 22

The drive to Crystal Mountain seemed to take forever. The girls had no idea where their mom was taking them, and none of them would even ask. There was an odd silence in the car. Everyone was tense. Dawn was smoking one cigarette after another.

Two hours later, they pulled into the Crystal Mountain parking lot. There were only a few cars there as it was off-season for skiing. Dawn didn't recognize any of the cars. She turned off the motor and they waited in silence.

Tom was watching for Dawn from inside the lodge. As she pulled in with her car, he waited for about ten minutes to be sure she wasn't followed. Seeing the coast was clear he walked out of the lodge and over to Dawn's car. He opened the passenger's car door and got in.

"Hello Dawn. Hello girls," Tom said softly.

"Hello Daddy!" the girls all said.

"Hello Tom," Dawn said.

"Just hello, Tom. What no kiss for your husband?" Tom said taunting Dawn.

"Tom, we're divorced." Remembering what Captain Potter had told her, Dawn leaned over and gave Tom a kiss.

"Now that's better. Come with me. I've got my car over there and Dawn, don't get cute. By the way Scott's not here. You'll see him when we get there," Tom said.

They followed Tom over to his car. When everyone's seatbelt was fastened Tom started the car and turned to Dawn. "I expect you won't try anything, or should I tie you up?"

"No, I won't try anything. I just want to see Scott."

Looking at the girls in the back seat Tom said, "It's going to be a long trip, so you girls might want to get some sleep." Then turning to Dawn, Tom said, "You look like hell. A couple of

167

hours would do you some good too."

Dawn just looked at Tom and made no response. Then Tom said, "I mean it, Dawn, close your eyes and try to get some sleep. Don't worry, Dear, I'm not going anywhere. I've waited a couple of years to get my family back. We'll never be apart again."

Knowing not to push Tom after all the years of being married to him, Dawn settled back in her seat and closed her eyes. *"I won't go to sleep, but I will try to rest. Dakota, I wish you could help me now,"* she thought to herself.

Looking out his window on the airplane, Dakota could see the airport was now in sight. As the plane started to make its descent, Dakota's phone rang. "Agent Deer here."

"Agent Deer, this is Agent Grolier. The team is waiting for you off of Canadian Highway 17. We're five miles east of Marathon. You'll see a black Ford Taurus sitting alongside the road at mile marker sixty. Agent Hunter will be there waiting to bring you to the team, Sir."

"Thank you, Agent Grolier."

"Agent Grolier out, Sir."

"Agent Deer out."

As the plane was taxing up to the terminal, Dakota could see the car and a special agent waiting for him. When the plane came to a stop, Dakota was up and at the door before the pilots even had time to get out of their seats.

Going down the stairs, Dakota could see someone he recognized standing by the car. A smile crossed the other man's face as he crossed his arms.

Walking up to the man Dakota said, "Well I'll be damned."

"And then some," Harold said to Dakota.

"Harold what are you doing here?" Dakota asked.

Harold smiled and said, "Seems to me you called Colonial Williams and said you needed the best. Well, Colonial Williams called and talked to the President. The President called me and pulled me out of retirement. I guess you could say, he thought you needed someone here that could keep you in line."

"Thanks for coming, Harold. Shall I drive, old man?"

"Do you still know how?" Harold asked with a grin.

"I'll give it a whirl," Dakota said and smiled.

Going down the highway, Dakota was watching the satellite scanning for Dawn and the girls' position.

"Dakota, maybe I should drive and then you can watch the screen," Harold said. Dakota looked up at Harold. "Son, they are behind us, which is just where we want them for now. Take a deep breath Dakota, we've got a long night ahead of us."

"Harold it's just that..." Dakota broke off.

"I know Dakota, no amount of training can prepare you for something like this. Just remember one thing. Every man out there knows this is your family. They are thinking to themselves, 'What if this was my family.' You've got the best out there and they'll be better than their best because of it," Harold said as he patted Dakota's shoulder.

It wasn't long before they spotted a black Ford by mile marker sixty. Dakota pulled over behind the car. He got out and walked up to the car. The man rolled down his car window. "Thanks for stopping Sir, but I have help on the way."

"Really? And I thought you were supposed to help me, Agent Hunter," Dakota said.

"Agent Deer? Sir, you wouldn't believe how many people have stopped to offer help," Agent Hunter answered him.

"It's good to know that citizens still care enough to help each other. I'll follow you, Agent Hunter."

"Yes sir, Agent Deer."

Dakota got back into his car, then looking at Harold he said, " It's only a short trip from here and then we'll be with the special forces team."

"Good, I'm getting too old for all this traveling in one day." Harold smiled.

Dakota picked up his cell phone and called Agent Potter.

"Agent Potter here," Chew said.

"Chew, it's Dakota. How far behind Dawn are you?"

"About two miles, Dakota. What's your location?"

"We're about to reach the team just outside Marathon," Dakota answered him.

"It's going to be about four hours before we're there. Everything is going as planned. Get set up and keep me posted for further instructions," Chew said.

"Will do, Agent Deer out."

"Agent Potter out."

Dakota and Harold followed Agent Hunter a few more miles and then turned off the highway onto a side road. From there they took a two-track into the woods about a mile off the road. In the clearing they could see the special forces team waiting.

Trying to have a sense of humor Dakota said, "Well Harold, it looks like the gang is all here."

"Yep, it looks like there's a party going on. Must be only black attire is allowed and I forgot my tux. Think they'll still let me in?" Harold said, smiling at Dakota.

As Dakota and Harold walked over to the group of men, Agent Ramsey spoke up. "Good to see you Agent Deer and Agent Green."

"Hello Agent Ramsey." Dakota then nodded his head towards the men. "Gentleman, I know you've been briefed on the situation at hand. I want to thank each one of you for your help in this matter."

"Agent Deer, we've sent out scouts to the Lake Nipigon area. They reported back to us that they have located your son with a lady. They are at a cabin about ten miles from here. It appears that your son is unharmed and that the lady is being friendly towards him. We feel at this time he is in no danger. We've taken pictures of the lady and sent them to CIA headquarters and are awaiting a reply as to her identity. We have mapped out the area and the location of the cabin," Agent Ramsey said as he showed Dakota the map.

"Well done, Agent Ramsey. Men, we need to set up around the cabin and wait. A man name Tom Brown will be showing up at the cabin tonight, most likely in the next few hours. He will have with him my wife and three daughters. If he should show any threat to any of my family, the sharp shooters have my permission to take him out. Although, I would rather have him alive and only injured. Please keep this in mind," Agent Deer told them.

"What about the lady, Agent Deer?" Harold asked.

"If she seems to be a threat to any of them, only shoot to injure her. Men, you know the drill on this kind of thing so I'm not going to go over that with you. If there are no further questions let's move out," Dakota said to the group.

Chapter 22

"So how was your nap, Dear?" Tom asked Dawn. Yawning, Dawn looked around her. Seeing the girls asleep in the back seat, she then turned to Tom. "Where are we? How long has it been dark?" she asked.

"A while now. Don't worry, it won't be long and we'll be there. I really hope you'll like our new home."

"Our new home? Tom, what are you talking about?"

"Dawn, I know I should have listened to you years ago, but now we have a second chance." Taking his hand and patting hers, he continued. "Where we're going no one will ever bother us again. I love you Dawn. Nothing will ever change that. I know at first it will be different for you, but Darling, you'll get used to it. I've lived in hell for two years without you and well, Dear if I can't have you, then I'll make sure no one does."

"Tom, what are you saying?" Dawn asked nervously

"Honey, when we took our marriage vows, it was for better or worse, until *death* do us part. The way I see it, we've been living through the better or worse part. The next time we split it will only be through death," Tom said firmly.

Dawn sucked in a breath of air, as if she were drowning. She knew Tom was crazy and would really do it. *"He's going to kill me,"* she thought.

The lights from the dash of the car gave enough illumination so that Tom could see the look of fear on Dawn's face. Taking her hand into his, he gave it a little squeeze. "Now don't worry Honey, I'm not going to hurt you. That is, as long as you don't ever try to leave me again. If you do, well I guess... I'll just have to kill you. By the way don't get any ideas, it's over fifty miles to the nearest neighbor."

Tom released Dawn's hand and she quickly pulled it away and crossed her arms onto her lap. She looked out the car window into the darkness and the tears rolled down her cheeks. As the tears fell from Dawn's cheeks they landed on Dakota's ring, she looked down at it. *"Dakota if only there was a way you could help us,"* Dawn thought to herself.

It was a foggy evening and visibility was nonexistent, which made seeing the special forces team spread throughout the woods next too impossible. It was a perfect night for such a mission. Looking through his infrared binoculars at the cabin, Dakota could see the dimly lit gasoline light sitting on the end table by the couch. A woman was sitting on the couch watching the fire with her back towards Dakota. When the woman got up, she leaned over, causing her long hair to cover her face. As she stood up, Dakota could see she had a sleeping boy in her arms. Relieved to see it was Scott, Dakota let out a sigh. The lady walked out of the room, but was back in about five minutes. She walked to the front french doors, looking out into the darkness of the night. It was then Dakota could see her face.

"Oh my God!" Dakota whispered.

"What is it, what's wrong Dakota?" Harold asked.

"I know that woman. Her name is Liz Gleason," Dakota whispered to Harold as he handed Harold the binoculars.

Looking at Liz, Harold said, "So what would she be doing here?"

"I'm not really sure," Dakota said stumped.

"Well the night is young and quiet, so go on, I want to hear this," Harold said handing the binoculars back to Dakota.

"To make a long story short. Years ago she came to see me when I was first in jail. We had a relationship that I cut off. You know, life sentence and all. For years she was Dawn's best friend that was until..." Dakota said looking through the binoculars.

"Until what?" Harold asked.

"Until...years later Dawn and I started writing, fell in love and well...you know the rest of the story," Dakota said still keeping an eye on Liz.

"You mean to tell me that this Liz person couldn't handle the fact that you and Dawn...."

"Yep, that's right, it broke up Dawn and Liz's friendship. Guess Liz couldn't handle the fact that what her and I had was back when she was eighteen and I was twenty. I had a life sentence. What was I supposed to do, ask her to wait twenty to thirty years? Four years later she married someone else," Dakota said.

"So that explains how Liz would know Tom. She must have known Tom while Dawn and him were married," Harold said. "How long has the friendship between the ladies been over?"

"A little over a year," Dakota said taking the binoculars away from his eyes.

"So... it all makes sense now," Harold said.

"What are you talking about?" Dakota asked looking at Harold.

"Dakota, you're really a top notch agent but when it comes to women and love...you, my boy, are lost in space. Liz hates Dawn because of you. Tom, I'm sure, knows about the man in prison that Dawn's in love with, thanks to Liz of course. Then we have our sick friend Tom, who wants the children back. Liz is more than willing to help Tom with his scheme, thus getting Dawn out of the way and hurting you for not loving Liz anymore. It's called revenge Dakota," Harold said.

"My God, they're going to kill Dawn," Dakota hissed.

Putting his hand on Dakota's shoulder, Harold said, "Not a chance, we're here. I'll be right back." Harold left Dakota and walked so quiet in the woods that even Dakota with his well-trained ear couldn't hear him walking.

When Harold returned about thirty minutes later Dakota asked him, "What were you doing?"

"Just making sure everyone was clear on what to do," Harold assured him.

Chapter 23

The car pulled onto the two-track and was heading for the cabin. The special forces team was ready and watching.

Tom stopped the car in front of the cabin, turned to Dawn and said, "Honey, welcome to our new home. I know you and the children will be happy here. It's late and I think we should get the girls to bed."

Knowing she had to play along with what Tom wanted, Dawn looked in the back seat, at the girls still asleep and said, "Yes Tom, I think you're right, it was a long trip and everyone's tired."

Helping the children out of the car, they walked up to the cabin. "Well, what do you think?" Tom said to Dawn.

Not really knowing what to say Dawn said, "I'd like to have a better look in the morning. It's really too dark out to tell, but from what I can see, it looks inviting." Seeing that Tom smiled at her answer, Dawn was relieved. She knew not to upset him.

As they walked into the cabin, Dawn spotted Liz sleeping on the couch. She looked at Tom, "What is she doing here?"

"We'll put the girls to bed and then we'll talk. I'll show you their room. Scott should be asleep in his room. We'll check on him too," Tom said softly.

Dawn wanted to check on Scott, so she forgot about Liz at the moment. "After that, I'd like to have some coffee, if you don't mind," Dawn said trying to sound normal.

Pleased that Dawn was taking things so well, Tom said, "Sure, or we could have a glass of wine if you'd like."

They tucked the girls into bed and then checked on Scott who was fast asleep. As far as Dawn could tell Scott looked content. Seeing that no harm had come to her son, Dawn relaxed a little.

Walking into the kitchen, they came upon Liz sitting at the

kitchen table drinking a cup of coffee. Liz got up, walked over to Tom and kissed him passionately on the lips, "Hello Darling, I missed you." Then to Dawn she said, "Hello Dawn, glad you could make it. I hope you like our little home. Too bad you won't be staying long."

Tom gave Liz a shove, "Shut up Liz. I need to talk to Dawn."

"What...but Tom," Liz said in shock.

"You heard me shut the hell up, I need to think..." Tom said full of anger.

"But Tom you told me..." Liz said

"I know what the hell I told you. Go to bed Liz, I'll talk to you in the morning," Tom ordered.

Liz walked past Tom and then pushed Dawn aside with her shoulder. "I won't be seeing you in the morning," she sneered.

As Dawn sized up the situation she knew her life was on the line. Dawn walked up to Tom; slipped her arm through his and said to Liz, "Don't count on it, Tom and I will be very happy here. After all this is the cabin that we planned together years ago."

Liz glared back at Dawn and said, "We'll see about that!" And she left the room.

Tom then walked with Dawn over to a chair at the table, "Here sit down, we really do need to talk," he said gently. Sitting down, Dawn watched Tom as he took a seat at the end of the table.

"Dawn, did you really mean that?" Tom asked

"What Tom?"

"What you said to Liz?"

Dawn turned to look out the window behind her, hoping to buy some time, "The cabin, from what I've seen so far, is just like what we talked about years ago."

"Do you really think you could be happy here?" Tom said placing his hand on Dawn's.

Turning back to look at Tom, Dawn's eye caught sight of

Liz standing in the door way with a gun pointing at Dawn. "Ta...Ta...Tom...Look...!" Dawn said and then froze.

Tom turned to look and saw Liz standing there with a gun pointing at Dawn. "What the hell are you doing?"

"I'm going to get rid of her once and for all. It's what we planned," Liz yelled as she pulled the gun up. In that same instant Tom jumped up, a shot rang out, the window behind Dawn broke, and Dawn slumped in her chair and then fell to the floor.

Liz dropped the gun and ran from the kitchen. As she ran down the hall she stopped at Scott's room went in and grabbed Scott. Then Liz ran out the front door with Scott and headed for her car. They were almost there when Liz came face to face with Dakota. "Let the boy go, Liz!" Dakota ordered, as he grabbed her, causing her to release Scott.

"Run Scott! Run!" Dakota yelled

Scott started to run and then stopped when he realized whose voice he had heard. He turned to look back and seen Dakota standing there by Liz. "Dad?"

"What are you doing here?" Liz asked as she slowly reached into her pocket and pulled out a small pistol shooting point blank at Dakota.

Dakota dropped to the ground. Another shot rang out and Liz dropped the gun and fell to the ground.

Everything happened in a split second, soon there were men everywhere. Scott ran over to Dakota and knelt down beside him. "Dad wake up, Dad..."

Someone's hand touched Scott's shoulder. "Scott, come with me. Let the doctors take care of him."

"No, I want to stay with my dad!" Scott screamed as the tears rolled down his face.

"My name is Harold, I'm your dad's friend and a police officer. You'll be safe with me," Harold said, reaching his hand out to Scott.

Scott looked back at Dakota lying there so still, "I love you,

Dad. Don't die. Please don't die." Taking Harold's hand Scott allowed Harold to lead him back to the cabin.

The girls were sitting in the living room with three members of the special forces team with them. As the men were talking to the girls and calming them down, Harold and Scott walked in. Scott ran over to his sisters sitting on the couch.

"Where's my mom?" Scott asked the men.

"She's in the kitchen, she's got a few cuts from the broken glass, but she's all right. The medic is in there now with her cleaning her cuts. She'll be out here in a few minutes," Agent Hunter told him.

"I'll go check on her, Scott. You stay here with your sisters and I'll be right back," Harold said.

"Promise you'll be right back?" Scott asked him.

"I promise within five minutes." Harold smiled at him.

The scene in the kitchen was gruesome; Tom was lying on the table in a pool of blood. Glass was all over the table and the floor. Dawn was lying motionless on the floor. Harold could see the medications were working on Dawn.

Walking over to where Dawn was, Harold asked the medics, "How is she?"

"She'll be fine Sir, just a few cuts from the glass. Looks like there's a nasty bump on her head. I'm sure when the drugs wear off, she'll have one nasty headache. She's starting to come around now," the medic answered.

"And what about him?" Harold asked looking at Tom.

"He's dead, Sir. Bullet went through his heart," Agent Jones answered.

Harold walked back out to the living room where the children were. "Your mom is going to be fine. She's got just a few cuts from the window breaking. Nothing big, and I think she might have a slight headache, but other than that she's fine. She'll be out here with you children in a few minutes."

"Sir, what about my dad?" Scott asked.

"I'm sorry, but your father was shot. He didn't make it,"

Harold said.

"I didn't see any blood on Daddy Dakota. He can't be dead," Scott said looking at the girls and then towards Dawn as a medic was helping her into the living room. Going over to his Mom Scott said, "Mom, Daddy Dakota is here, Liz shot him out by the car, but I didn't see any blood, so he can't be dead."

"What...Dakota's here, how can that be?" Dawn said.

"Mom, he saved me. Liz was going to take me away, but Daddy Dakota stopped her and told her to let me go. Then she shot him. He's here Mom, I knelt down beside him," Scott insisted.

The medic helped Dawn sit down into a chair. Rubbing her head Dawn said, "Scott, Dakota's in prison, he can't be here."

"Ma'am, maybe I can explain things," Harold said.

Everyone looked at Harold. "I'm not sure who this Dakota person is your son is referring to, but it must be that one of our men resembles him. After all it is dark out and things happened so fast. Under the circumstances a child would want someone they trust to be there. I truly believe that your son was so scared that he wished for this Dakota person when really it was one of my men that saved him," Harold explained.

Dawn looked at Scott, "You know it does make sense what this man says. I think maybe you wished for Dakota so hard that you thought he was here. We all wish he were here."

Outside Chew was shaking Dakota. As Dakota started to catch his breath Chew grabbed his arm to help him up, "Dakota, get up man, before they find you out here."

"That bitch knocked the wind right out of me," Dakota said looking at Liz lying on the ground.

"Yea, well she won't be shooting at anyone ever again. It's a good thing you had your bullet proof vest on or we would be going to your funeral," Chew said.

His senses coming back to him, Dakota said, "My God, she shot Dawn!" As Dakota slipped out of Chew's grip, he turned to run towards the house. Chew grabbed his arm again, "Whoa, wait a minute, you can't go in there!"

"Dawn's been shot! The hell I can't!" Dakota yelled.

"She's fine, it was only a drug dart," Chew said as he tackled Dakota to the ground.

"What?" Dakota looked at him

"Trust me, Dakota, she's fine. I'll explain it all to you, but let's get out of here and under some cover so we're not seen," Chew said.

Knowing Chew wouldn't lie to him about something like that, Dakota agreed to go with him. "This had better be good," Dakota said to Chew.

Once back in the woods and out of sight Chew radioed to Harold, "Agent Green, this is Agent Potter. Sir, I have a problem out here I think you need to address."

Hearing this through the transmitter in his ear, Harold said, "Excuse me I have a few things to check on outside. Ma'am, you and the children will be safe with these men. Everything's under control." Once outside Harold radioed back to Agent Potter. "Agent Potter where are you?"

"Keep walking north, Sir, we see you," Agent Potter answered.

When he reached them, Dakota said, "Ok Harold, first of all how are Dawn and the children, and what the hell happened?"

"They are all fine. Now calm down Dakota," Harold answered him.

"You want me to calm down! I saw that bitch shoot my wife, and you want me to calm down?" Dakota said upset.

"Liz didn't shoot Dawn. One of our men did with a drug dart it was under my orders. Remember, when I walked away from you? I gave instructions to several of our sharp shooters to load up with drug darts. If someone in the cabin threatened to kill Dawn. Dawn was to be shot with a drug dart. Therefore taking her out of the equation. Then the other sharp shooters were to take out whoever was threatening her. It just so happens Tom got the bullet from Liz's gun that was meant for

Dawn. Dawn is fine. A few cuts from the broken glass, and I imagine a nasty headache from hitting the floor, but she's just fine. The medics have checked her out. The children are a little shook up, but everyone's fine. Now you need to get the hell out of here, Scott swears he's seen you," Harold ordered.

"Not until I have a look just to make sure." Dakota insisted.

"Fine, let him go, Agent Potter," Harold said, then turning to Dakota, "Son, you stay out of sight! Take a look at your family and then get your ass back here. Make it quick, you need to get back to prison before someone here finds out who and what you really are."

Dakota walked close enough to the house from the woods that he could see Dawn and the children through the window. *"Thank God, they're all fine,"* he said to himself. Standing there watching them, he longed to be with them. *"Honey, I'm right here watching over you. Things will be fine."*

Right then Dawn stood up, walked over to the window and looked out into the darkness. She took her hand brought it to her lips and blew a kiss out the window. *"I don't understand how Dakota, but I know you're here,"* she said to herself.

Chew walked up to Dakota, "You ok, Dakota?"

Dakota looked at Chew, "She knows I'm close. She feels it here," Dakota said moving his hand and laying it across his heart. "She just blew me a kiss."

Chew looked towards the cabin and saw Dawn standing by the window. "She's going to be fine. I think we'd better go. Your time together will come."

As they started to walk away Dakota stopped and took one more look at Dawn. "Somehow, some way, some day, we'll be together," he said as he took his hand and blew her a kiss back.

Chapter 23

A year later....

As Dawn was sound a sleep, the nightmare reoccurred once again. She found herself sitting at the table, with her back to the picture window. She was in the kitchen at the cabin in Canada.

Twelve hundred miles away at the police barracks in Louisiana, Dakota was having the same dream. He was on the edge of the woods looking into the cabin.

The alarm going off brought Dakota out of his dream. As he reached over to turn it off, he missed the button and knocked the alarm on the floor.

"And good morning to you too," he said as he reached to the floor to turn off the alarm.

Turning back over on the bed Dakota stared up into the darkness. His thoughts drifted back to Dawn. She was the love of his life and it was hell being apart from her and the children. They needed him and he needed them. "Only three more years and my contract with the government will be up. Shit, might as well be a life sentence. A lot could happen in three years, Honey, just hang in there and wait," He said into the silence.

Getting out of bed, Dakota got dressed, brushed his teeth and walked out to the kitchen to get a cup of coffee. Looking at his watch and knowing it was near time for Dawn to be getting up, he couldn't resist the temptation to call her.

The phone on the other end was ringing, a very sleepy voice answered.

"Hello," Dawn said with a yawn.

"Good morning, Darling, the sun is up, well almost. It's a beautiful day out, or should I say is going to be, and I'm calling to tell you how much I love you."

"Dakota, I love waking up and hearing your voice. It makes

all my days wonderful and I love you too!"

"And how did my baby sleep last night?" Dakota asked Dawn.

"Oh...all right I guess," Dawn answered him.

Dakota sensed the hesitation in Dawn's voice when she answered. "Dawn what's wrong?"

"Nothing really," she said shyly.

"Come on Dawn, I can hear it in your voice what's bothering you?" he coxed her.

"I was just dreaming about when Tom kidnapped the kids and me. I know I should be over it by now, it's been a year, but sometimes it just comes back to me in my dreams. But really, I'm fine," she said.

"Honey if I could change that time in your life, trust me I would. Tom will never hurt you again. Tom and Liz are dead. And as God as my witness, Darling, no one will ever hurt you or the children again! You can well-bet I'll see to that," Dakota said with passion.

"Dakota, I know when the children and I came down to see you in prison it really bothered you...but it's been a year and a half...and well..."

Dakota interrupted her, "I need to see you too, Honey."

There was silence on the other end. "Dawn, you there?"

"Yes," she said barley a whisper.

"I've been giving it a lot of thought, and well maybe if you came down, it would help the bad dreams stop. If nothing else, it would give us both some happy thoughts," Dakota said sweetly.

Dawn perked up. "When Dakota?"

"Oh, I don't know. I was thinking yesterday would have been pretty good," he teased. "As soon as you can. Only... Dawn?"

"I'm here." She held her breath.

"This time I want to see you alone. It's not that I don't love the kids; you know I do, but this time needs to be for us. I'm at the state police barracks and we'll have a little more freedom than before at the prison. Is that all right with you?" he asked hoping she would understand.

"I agree, I'll take the kids to Kentucky and they can spend the time with Aunt Nancy. I know she won't mind and they'll have a good time. I need this time alone with you too," Dawn answered excited.

"Well Darling, I know you have to get ready for work, so I should let you go for now. I'll be thinking about you," he said with love in his voice.

"I love you, Dakota! I'll get a hold of Nancy tonight and when you call me next, I'll let you know when I'm coming down."

"Dawn, I know this may be pushing things for you, but I want you to spend the night with me," Dakota said, wondering what she would say to that.

"What! Really? They'll let me do that? How can that be Dakota?" Dawn said shocked.

"Don't worry about how, all I want to know, is will my darling wife stay the weekend with me? I promise I won't push anything on you. That's not what I'm about. I just want to spend time with you," Dakota said with sincerity.

"Yes, I'll spend the weekend with you, did you really have to ask? I also know very well that you're not that way, but Dakota, I'd be lying to you if I said a thing or two doesn't cross my mind," Dawn said.

Laughing Dakota said, "Look Darling, I'm not a saint. I'll admit, I've had thoughts, but I just want you to know I'll never push you. When the time is right, things will happen. But Dawn, it has to be right for both of us. Now let me let you go. Give the kids my love and know I love you too!"

"I love you Dakota, I can't wait to see you."

"Dawn, be a dear and hang up the phone," Dakota said

"O.K. I'll talk to you later." And with that she hung up the phone.

Later that day Dakota went to see the captain at the state police barracks. As he walked into the captain's office, he could see the captain was in deep thought. He quietly walked up to the desk and sat down in one of the chairs in front of it. It was five minutes before the captain looked up and even realized Dakota was there.

"Dakota, I'll never get use to fact that you move as quiet as a mouse," Captain Miller said.

Smiling at the Captain Dakota said, "That's what they train me for, Sir."

Sitting back in his chair Captain Miller said, "So what can I do for you, Dakota?"

"I have a request, Sir," Dakota said calmly.

"And what might that be?" Captain Miller asked.

"My wife will be coming down to visit me and I want to request a special visit," Dakota said with a smile.

"That's not a problem Dakota, arrangements were made for you before when she visited you at the prison," Captain Miller said.

"Well Sir, I mean a really special visit. I want her to stay the weekend with me at my apartment, here at the barracks," Dakota said, ready for the captain to blow on that one.

Standing up, putting both his hands on the desk, Captain Miller leaned over and said, "Have you gone MAD? What in the Hell do you mean you want her to stay here at the barracks? In case you haven't noticed Dakota, this is a CORRECTION'S FACILITY! Hell, why not just invite the whole damn family, and just have a family reunion? NO, way Dakota and that's my final answer!"

Sitting calmly in his chair and smiling at the captain, Dakota said, "Do you really know what you're saying?"

Having heard Dakota ask him this question before and knowing World War Three was ready to break out, but knowing the answer still had to be no, the Captain answered, "Yes Dakota, I know what I'm saying. There's no way I can pull something like that off."

Leaning forward in his chair, Dakota put his elbows on the desk. Looking the captain in his eyes, he said, "I will have my wife here and she will stay the weekend with me! I will be leaving in three months on a mission that will have me out of the states for a year. I won't be able to have any contact with my wife by letter or phone during that time. Pretty much I'm going to have to break my wife's heart and cut her out of my life, but before I do that, I'm going to show her more love than she's seen in a lifetime. If I'm lucky, that love will pull us through. Meanwhile, I don't give a damn what you have to do to make this happen. But you will do it! Now if you need help with this, I'm sure we can contact the governor and the President. Maybe then, you can explain to them why their top agent can't have such a simple thing as spending the weekend with his wife!"

Captain Miller sat down and put his head in his hands. "I knew the day would come that having an agent for the U.S. government pose as an inmate with a life sentence would be a problem." Looking back up at Dakota, the captain continued, "I don't think we need to go that far. Just how in the sam hell am I going to explain to the other twenty inmates on why your wife is here, when they can't have a visit such as this?"

"Maybe you should get rid of them, then what they don't know, won't hurt them?" Dakota said.

"What a grand idea, maybe I should just give them all a weekend pass. You know the honor system. What do you think from six p.m. on Friday to let's say six p.m. on Sunday? I'm sure they'd all come back," Captain Miller said.

Shaking his head Dakota said, "Why not send them all back to the prison? Say I came down with something really contagious, keep them up there oh say a week or so, that should be enough time to cover most anything I might have."

Looking back up at Dakota, Captain Miller said. "You know Dakota, that just might not be such a bad idea. It's a believable story. We wouldn't be able to send you back to the prison; after all, you might spread it like wildfire to the other inmates. We'd have to keep you here to keep the sickness confined. So when are we going to do this?"

Standing up and turning to walk away, Dakota looked back at the captain. "I'll let you know." With that he walked out of the office.

Walking towards his wood shop, Dakota had Dawn on his mind and didn't see Chew leaning against the building. "I think I'll make something special for my wife today. I want her to remember our special weekend together and when she looks at it, she'll feel the love I have for her," he said out loud talking to himself.

"Really, and what might that be?" Chew said bringing Dakota out of his daydream.

"Hey Chew, I didn't even see ya there, bro."

"No kidding? A land mind could have been in front of you Dakota and more than likely you would have walked right on it," Chew said seriously.

"What can I say Chew, I had a little filly up north on my mind? Why don't you come on in the wood shop and I'll fix us some coffee. I've got a few things on my mind I want to talk to you about."

As Dakota was making a pot of coffee, Chew watched him with concern on his mind. It wasn't like Dakota to let his guard down, he was always aware of what was around him. When Dakota looked up at Chew and seen the concern look on his face he asked, "What's wrong Chew?"

"Why don't you tell me Dakota? It's not like you to be off in space somewhere. Of all the agents I know, you're always on your toes. If Dawn has got you this messed up, it could cost you your life and maybe others as well."

"That's one thing I like about you Agent Potter, you don't beat around the bush. You get right to the point."

"No Dakota, I haven't got to the point yet, that was sugar

coating it. If you'd like me to get to the point I can though."

"Do I have a choice here? Might as well get it off your mind Chew, I'm all ears!" Dakota said with his guard up.

"Ever since you got involved with Dawn, you've had agents watching her and the children, twenty-four seven. Your head's in the clouds. You're doing your job half-assed and putting a lot of us in danger. You can't handle *love* and being an agent at the same time Dakota! Ditch the bitch," Chew said.

No more than Chew got the words out, Dakota snapped and was swinging his fist at Chew. The first impact was on Chew's face, then another hit in his stomach. The first two hits were shock and disbelief for Chew, and then natural instinct to fight back came into play. Before long they were swinging and fighting all over the wood shop. Table saws, wood planers, and wood tools were knocked all over the place. As Chew fell to the floor, Dakota was on top of him, with a hammer in his hand, getting ready to hit Chew. Dakota's senses came back to him. He dropped the hammer got off of Chew and stumbled away.

Catching his breath Dakota said, "Ma... Ma... Man ...I'm sorry, I don't know what came over me. Are you all right, Chew?"

Lying there, catching his breath Chew said, "You're losing your grip Dakota, where the hell are you?"

Shaking his head Dakota answered him, "Man, I'm all fucked up."

"You're telling me. What are you going to do Dakota? You can't keep going on like this," Chew said.

"That's what I wanted to talk to you about. Dawn is coming down to spend the weekend with me. I've made arrangements for her to stay here at the barracks in my apartment with me. You know I'm leaving the country in three months. I'll be gone a year. I know I can't have any contact with her, not by letter or phone. I want to keep the agents watching her and the children.

"I was going to ask you to handle things for me while I'm gone. I love her Chew, and yes I know I'm going to break her heart, but before I do, I have to show her the love I really hold for her. It's driving me crazy. God, she doesn't deserve this," he said shaking his head.

Understanding what Dakota must be feeling, Chew said, "You know I'll take care of it. Not that this will make you feel any better, but if the love you two share is strong enough, it'll last through this and beyond. You have to trust her love for you Dakota."

Walking back over to where Chew was still laying on the floor, Dakota reached out and offered him his hand. Chew reached up and they locked hands, with one jerk, Chew was back up on his feet.

Putting their arms around each other, Dakota said, "Thanks man, you ok?"

"I'll heal quicker than you will, you sorry Yankee."

"That's 'cause I don't eat all those pig guts, that's sure to kill anything," Dakota said laughing.

"So what is it you're going to make for this little lady?" Chew asked.

Looking at the mess in the wood shop, Dakota answered him, "Maybe, we should clean this place up and then I'll have to think about it."

Later that evening, Dawn called Kentucky to talk to her friend Nancy.

"Oh Nancy, I can't thank you enough for helping me out this way. I know the kids will have a great time at your house."

"I told you before girl, that there was something special about Dakota. I still wonder Dawn, how a man in prison can know and do the things he does. Give me a call next Wednesday before you leave. Plan on staying the night here, don't go and think you can drive twenty-one hours straight through. You know I'm at the halfway point on your trip. Do you plan on staying in Baton Rouge on Thursday night?"

"Yes, I thought if I left your house on Thursday morning, then I could get to Baton Rouge early Thursday evening, get a good night's sleep, well try too anyway. Then Friday morning I'd go over to the state police barracks and find out where Dakota's apartment is."

"So tell me Dawn, which one of you is going to sleep on the couch?" Nancy teased her.

"Well if he's truly a southern gentleman, Miss Nancy, I'm sure it won't be me," Dawn teased back.

"Oh I see, so you think the man's going to give up his bed? More like he'll share it with you," Nancy said playfully.

"Well, time will tell Mizz Nancy. Guess, I'll let you go for now. Thanks again."

"Anytime, you know I enjoy the kids. Take care and tell Dakota I said hi."

"Bye for now," Dawn said.

"See ya," Nancy said as she hung up the phone.

The children were going through their nightly routines, getting ready for bed. Everyone wanted the bathroom all at once.

"Mom, the girls keep taking cuts. When one goes in, the other two follow. They take forever in there," Scott said.

Lou opened the bathroom door just enough to poke her head out. "Stop your whining, if you were a girl you wouldn't have this problem," with that said she stuck her tongue out at him and closed and locked the door.

Scott started beating on the door. "You'd better open this door and get out of there before I break it down!" he yelled.

"Scott, stop that before you break the door. Girls, get out of the bathroom and let your brother in there!" Dawn said sternly.

The door to the bathroom quickly opened and Scott lunged forward, not expecting it to open so fast. In the next few seconds he was greeted with glasses of water from his three sisters.

"There that should cool you off," Lynn said laughing. Scott

grabbed a glass from his sister Leigh, made his way to the bathroom sink. Filling his glass, the girls ran out of the bathroom screaming. Having his glass full of ammunition, Scott ran out of the bathroom, down the hall. Seeing a shadow peering from around the corner, Scott got ready to take aim. As he rounded the corner, he let the water fly, hitting his target right in the face.

"SCOTT TIMOTHY!" his mother yelled.

"Uh…Uh I thought you were the girls. I'm sorry, Mom. I was just going to pay them back. They got me all wet first!" Scott said.

"Girls, get out here. NOW!" Dawn said sternly.

Just then the phone rang, Lou ran to answer it. "I've got it," she said. Picking it up she answered so sweetly. "Hello."

"Good Evening, little Darling, and what is my youngest girl up to?" Dakota asked.

"Oh nothing." Lou said soundly like such a sweet angel. "But boy is Scott in trouble Daddy Dakota, he just threw water all over Mom," she added with excitement.

Dawn, hearing it was Dakota and reaching for a kitchen towel, looked at Lou and said, "Lou, why don't you tell your Daddy Dakota, why Mom's all wet!"

Dakota could hear what Dawn had said in the background. "Well Darling, is there something you want to tell me?"

"Not really Daddy," Lou said.

"LOU! You tell him, or I will!" Dawn said hearing what Lou had said to Dakota. Dakota heard the sharpness in Dawn's voice.

"Well Darling, Mom sounds like she's on the war path, might as well tell me what happened," Dakota said to Lou.

"It's not my fault Daddy, it's Lynn and Leigh's. They made me do it," Lou said, pleading with her voice.

"Do what?" Dakota asked with a fatherly tone.

"They had me open the bathroom door and stick my tongue out at Scott. Us girls were all in the bathroom and Scott wanted in. You should have heard him, Daddy. He was pounding on the door. Well we opened the door like he asked, and well he was so hot, we thought we'd cool him off. We threw water at him. We all ran out of the bathroom to our bedroom and locked the door, so Scott couldn't get us. Scott had a glass of water and ran down the hall, went around the corner and threw it at Mom. Guess he thought it was us around the corner. Anyway, Mom's all wet, but I don't think the water helped cool her off. She looks really hot," Lou told her Dad shyly.

Smiling, he was thinking to himself that this is what having a family is all about and he would have loved to have been there and seen that. Harmless childhood pranks which every parent gets upset with at the time, and then laughs about it years later. Taking the smile out of his voice he said, "Now you really expect me to believe that it was just Lynn and Leigh's idea, that you had nothing to do with any of this?"

"No…Daddy," Lou said pouting.

"Turn on the speaker phone Lou and tell you sisters and brother I want to talk to them," Dakota said.

"Lynn, Leigh and Scott, Dad wants to talk to us, were in trouble now!" Lou said with a panic in her voice.

As Dawn watched all four children gather around the speakerphone and the looks on their faces, she admired Dakota for taking on the children as if they were his own. She could see the love and respect the children had for Dakota as a father.

"Are we all here?" Dakota asked.

"Yes, Dad," they answered.

"Now to begin with, you don't have water fights in the house, you have them outside. Second, you'll clean up your mess, and tell your mom you're sorry. Scott, a young man doesn't lose his temper and bang on a door. Tomorrow, the four of you will go outside, rake the yard and make sure all the little sticks and rocks are picked up, while you're doing this, I want you all to think about how you acted in the house tonight. Now, go do what you have to do and get to bed. I love you all and I'll call tomorrow night," Dakota said sternly.

Hanging their heads they all told Dakota good night, cleaned up their mess apologized to their mother and went quietly to bed.

"Dawn, you there?" Dakota asked, still on the speakerphone. Taking the phone off of speaker, Dawn picked up the handset and answered him, "Yes, I'm still here."

"Honey, I know it's not funny what happened, but I sure would have loved to have seen it. Now that you've had your shower, tell me Darling, how was your day?" Dakota said laughing.

"You're really cute, Dakota!"

"Oh come on Honey, someday you'll look back on their little pranks and have a good laugh. As sweet as you are, I'm sure you did a few pranks here and there as a child that got you into trouble too. Bet you and your parents laugh about it now." Smiling, Dawn was thinking about a few tricks that her brothers and she had done. They got into trouble for it then, and as Dakota said, their parents and them laugh about it now. Continuing on Dakota said, "I was a good Dad, I punished them, the lawn's in a bad way for a raking, now it will get done." Shaking her head in agreement with him, the lawn defiantly needed a raking and then his last statement caught Dawn's attention.

"And just how would you know how bad the lawn is?" Dawn asked.

"Oh I just have my ways," he answered.

"Dakota are you sure you're locked up? I mean you seem to know a lot of things that go on around here, for being so far away."

"Well I'm either locked up or in the military, must be I'm locked up, cause you get a thirty-day leave a year in the military, and I don't get that here," he teased her.

"Dakota, I'm being serious."

"Honey, stop worrying about things that aren't important.

193

Just know I have a sixth sense when it comes to you and the children. Now tell me when you're coming to spend the weekend with your husband."

"You don't know how I wish that were true," Dawn said wishfully.

"What Darling?"

"That you were my husband and I was your wife. Dakota, I'd marry you in prison, I don't care how long you're there, I want to really be your wife," she said sadly.

Michigan, Dakota knew, no longer had common-law marriages, however they still recognized and honored other state's common-law marriages.

Knowing he couldn't tell her that according to the laws of Louisiana, that they were already common-law husband and wife, which was legally binding, and had been for over a year.

"Honey, just know in my heart, you are my wife, will always be my wife, nothing will ever change that. When I come home, we'll work this all out. I just want to know one thing, Darling. If you had to wait for me for a couple of years, could you do that?"

"Dakota, I could wait a lifetime for you. Even though I've been married before, I have never felt more love than I do from you."

Smiling at her answer Dakota said, "So back to my question, when is my Darling *wife* going to come spend the weekend with her husband?"

"Let's see, this is Sunday evening? Is next weekend too soon?" Dawn said trying to sound serious.

Not expecting that for her answer Dakota said, "Wow! You must really miss me. Can you get time off of work on that short of notice?"

"You'd be surprised the pull I have around WTLK. I have been pulling in some real whopper accounts, I'm sure they won't have a problem with it at all. Now if that's too soon for you I guess I could wait a month or two."

"No Ma'am, that will just be fine, in fact the next five days will be the longest in my life," he said happily.

"Dakota, is there anything you want me to bring for you?"

"Yes Ma'am, bring lots of pictures of you and the children, and along with that bring all your love."

"I'm being serious," Dawn answered him.

"So am I. Honey, I have everything I need. I'll have even more once you're here. Look, it's getting late so I should let you go to bed. I know you've already had your shower, thanks to Scott and the girls. I love you Dawn. Sweet dreams."

"Yes, it was rather a short and cold shower. I love you too." With that Dawn hung up the phone.

After Dakota hung up the phone, he walked out of his apartment and down to the wood shop. Once in the wood shop he looked through many of his patterns to see what he could make that would be special for his wife. Nothing was to his liking. He then sat on the stool by the workbench. Searching his mind on something special for Dawn, it came to him at last.

Going over to his cypress knees, Dakota sorted through them until he found just the right one. It was about three feet tall and twelve inches at the base. Looking it over and seeing the bark was still in good shape, he then took it over to his table saw. Laying it down, he cut it in half, lengthwise. Sanding the flat side of it smooth and blowing off the sawdust, he was now ready to draw on it.

A few hours later Dakota stood back and looked at his drawing. Now it was time for the verse from the bible.

I Corinthians 13:4,7,8
Love is long-suffering and kind.
It bears all things, believes all things
Hopes all things, endures all things.
Love never fails.

This verse he placed in the middle of the cypress knee.

Standing back and looking at the long stem rose and the white dove on either side of the verse, Dakota was satisfied. Tomorrow he'd start the wood burning and then the painting.

During the time he knew they'd be apart, he hoped Dawn would look at this and believe it in her heart. A year with no contact at all was going to be hard on them both, but mostly her, Dakota thought. He could only pray she wouldn't give up on their love.

It was now three in the morning and Dakota knew it was going to be another short night. Seven in the morning was going to come quick. Putting everything away he headed back to his apartment.

Tuesday evening, as Dawn was packing the children's things for their visit with Aunt Nancy, a knock could be heard at the door. "I'll get it," Scott said.

As Scott went to the door, he could see their neighbor, Donna. "Hello Scott," she said as she walked into the house. "Bet your mom's busy packing."

"Yep, I think she's packing us all for a year. A good thing we're taking the van. Mom's got coffee on."

"I thought she would, you know your mom and me, we can't live without our coffee," Donna said.

Donna walked to the kitchen, poured a cup of coffee, then asked Scott, "So which room is she packing up for the next year?"

"She's in the girls' room. She's already packed me for a year, maybe even two!" Scott said laughing. Donna started to walk towards the girls' room, and then turned back to Scott, "Do you think maybe I should offer to let her borrow my trailer, you know just in case she wants to take the kitchen sink?"

"Might not hurt to ask her," he said as he settled down on the couch to watch T.V.

As Donna leaned in the doorway with her coffee in hand she said, "Better pack their winter things, you know it could snow in the next six months."

Dawn was sitting on the floor with piles of clothes around her, as she looked up she smiled at Donna, "You know that might be a good idea. Got another cup of that coffee out there for me?"

"Sure do, just leave you fifty-cents by the pot, can you believe the cost of coffee now days? I can remember when it was a quarter a cup, but since you're going on a trip we'll just say it's on the house." Donna smiled.

Dawn stood up and tiptoed over the piles of clothes, "Guess I could use a break. I've got Scott and myself all packed, thought I'd leave the girls for last."

As the ladies walked out to the kitchen Donna headed for the coffee pot, "Sit down, I'll get you a cup."

"Thanks, Donna," Dawn said as she sat down at the kitchen table while Donna poured her a cup of coffee. As Donna put a little cream and sugar in Dawn's coffee she said, "So how are you doing?"

"I'm fine, a little tired maybe, but that's about it."

Walking back to the table with Dawn's coffee and giving it to her Donna said, "You don't look fine, in fact you look like you lost your best friend."

Taking a sip of her coffee and then looking at Donna, who now sat across from Dawn at the table she said, "No, nothing like that. I'm just a little nervous."

"Girl, what do you have to be nervous about? The man is in love with you, isn't he?" Donna said.

"Yes he is. Oh Donna, he shows me more love than I've ever had in my life."

"And...So what's the problem?"

"I'm not sure. I guess I feel like a high school girl in love for the first time. Well maybe not a high school girl, oh I don't know how to describe it," Dawn said flustered.

"Maybe the real problem is you're afraid he'll push sex on you, or make you feel like you have to. Could it be, it's crossed your mind that the man has been locked up for years, and just maybe you're afraid of that?" With the look on Dawn's face, Donna knew she hit the nail on the head.

Embarrassed, Dawn looked into her cup, "Well yes, I guess that's it. Am I being silly?"

"No, but if the man loves you as much as you say he does, you have nothing to worry about. Look deep into your heart Dawn and you'll find the answer there."

Thinking for a moment about what Donna was saying, Dawn knew what the real problem was. It wasn't Dakota she was afraid of, but herself. She had never had a man really make love to her, but had been abused with sex. She was afraid of her reaction if he touched her. Would she turn her feelings off, as she had done so much in the past? Would she lose the chance of knowing what intimacy between two people in love could be?

Donna broke the silence, "From the look on your face, I can see you found your answer."

"You're right I did. Thanks Donna."

Smiling at Dawn, Donna said, "What are friends for? So tell me, how much packing do you have left?"

"It's all sorted and ready to go into the suitcases," Dawn said proudly. "And I don't even need a trailer to haul it all in."

"Way to go girl! Now let's get it packed and I'll help you put it in the van. You need to get your sleep," Donna said.

"Thanks Donna."

As Dawn placed the last suitcase in the van and closed the door she said, "Well that should do it."

Donna laughed, "Are you sure? I don't remember bringing out the kitchen sink."

Smiling at Donna, Dawn said, "Oh that? I grabbed it on the last load, it's under the back seat."

"Well I think it's time for me to head on home. You have a safe trip," Donna said and she started to walk away.

"I will. Thanks again Donna."

"Oh, and Dawn," Donna said as she turned around to look at Dawn.

"Yea," Dawn answered.

With a wink and a smile Donna said, "Enjoy your visit. Really enjoy your visit."

"Smart-ass," Dawn said smiling as she walked back to the house.

The trip to Kentucky went well. The weather was perfect; the children were angels and hadn't even argued one time.

When they had arrived at Nancy's, she was thrilled to see Dawn and the children. Dawn and Nancy spent a nice evening talking, while the children watched movies on cable T.V.

Early the next morning, after Dawn has kissed each child goodbye, she walked out to the van with Nancy.

"Don't worry about a thing. The children will be no problem. You just have a great time with that man of yours," Nancy said.

"I can't tell you how much I appreciate this, Nancy," Dawn said as she got into the van.

"Dawn, you'd do the same for me. Besides, the kids love seeing each other again. Just remember to tell Dakota I'm charging him by the hour for babysitting."

"Wonder if he'll think I'm worth the bill," Dawn said laughing to Nancy.

"You'd better get going, you have a long trip ahead of you," Nancy said as she shut the door on the van.

Dawn started the van, "Thanks again, Nancy."

As Dawn made her way towards Louisiana, she daydreamed about Dakota. The thought of being alone with him made her heart sing. Deep into her thoughts Dawn didn't even notice the car merging onto the highway. The sound of the other car's horn snapped Dawn out of her daydream. She quickly swerved, her car missing the other car by only inches.

"Damn did you see that, Agent James? What's the matter with her?" asked Agent Maranda.

"I'm not sure. Maybe she's tired. We've got a few hours to go, hope she's going to be all right," Agent James answered him.

"She'd better be all right. I don't want to be the one to tell Agent Deer any bad news about that little lady. That man would come unglued, and you can well-bet heads would roll," said Agent Maranda.

"If you only knew," Agent James said.

A few hours later the phone in the agent's car was ringing. "Might as well answer that, we both know who it is," said Agent James.

"Agent Maranda, here," the Agent answered.

"Agent Maranda, this is Agent Deer. How's the trip going?" Dakota asked.

"Fine Sir. Were about an hour away from the barracks," replied Agent Maranda.

"Good, I'll be waiting," Dakota answered.

"Yes Sir, Agent Deer."

"Agent Maranda, I just want to thank you and Agent James for keeping a close eye on my wife and family," Dakota said.

"Your welcome Sir, Agent Maranda out." He then looked over at Agent James. "You're never going to believe this one. Agent Deer thanked us for watching his wife and family! Did you know she was his wife?" Agent Maranda said with total surprise.

"Yea kid, I knew. That little lady in front of us has no idea of the value she has to this country." Agent James looked at him and smiled.

"Sir, what do you mean? She doesn't even know we're following her and I know she has no idea that Agent Deer is an agent," Agent Maranda said puzzled.

"It's a long story, but here's the short version. Agent Deer isn't just a regular agent. He's this country's most valuable agent. Even the President doesn't question what Dakota, I mean Agent Deer wants to do. Keeping her safe keeps Agent

Deer happy and if he's happy then the country is a lot better off. Trust me kid, watching out for this lady's welfare is the best possible career move you could have made," Agent James said.

Looking back at the van in front of them and the lady driving it Agent Maranda said, "How long have you known Agent Deer? You sound like you know him on a personal level."

"Yea, something like that," Agent James said, smiling at Agent Maranda.

Agent Maranda knew that Agent James had been around and seen a lot of action, and that he had worked for the government for years. It was best not to question the senior agents too much, but to listen and learn from them was an advantage to any new agent.

Putting the finishing touches on the apartment, Dakota looked around and smiled. A knock at the door made Dakota's heart skip a beat. Walking over to the door, Dakota opened it surprised to see Chew.

"I think you forgot something," Chew said as he walked past Dakota to set the large cypress knee on the table.

"I was just making sure everything was perfect, how could I have forgotten that?" Dakota said.

"Wow, this place looks great. What, you on a honeymoon or something?" Chew teased.

"Something like that. I sure hope she feels the same way."

"Dakota, you worry too much. I think this will look great right here," placing the cypress knee in the middle of the coffee table, Chew stood back and looked at it. "Yep, she'll see it when she first walks in."

"Thanks, Chew."

Walking over to Dakota and placing his hand on Dakota's shoulder, Chew said, "Dakota, there's one thing I want you to keep in mind. The only thing the lady wants is you to be you. Fixing this apartment all up and making it romantic looking is great, but give the woman what she longs for the most." Then taking his hand and placing it on Dakota's chest, right above his heart. Chew continued, "Give her what's in here Dakota, that will last her a lifetime and she'll cherish it always."

"She already has that," Dakota said.

"I know, but show her. She's heard it and read it, now let her feel it," with that said Chew walked out of the apartment.

Looking up at the clock, Dakota picked up the phone and dialed it.

"Agent James here."

"John, where you at?"

"In my car Dakota, where else do you think I would be?" Agent James said.

"Smart-ass, how long before you're here?"

"The package is about ready to turn into the state police barracks. Light the candles and break out the wine, you have about two minutes," John said with a laugh.

"Thanks, John."

"No problem, Dakota. Agent James out." Looking at Agent Maranda, Agent James said, "Now that's one nervous agent. The honeymoon is about to begin."

Knowing sometimes it was better not to say anything, Agent Maranda just nodded as they watched Dawn park the van in front of the office. As she got out of the van and walked into the office Agent James said, "Well, we have the weekend off now. Our job is done until Monday morning."

As Dawn walked up to the counter in the office a lady stood there working on the computer, "I'll be with you in just a second." With a few more keystrokes and a smile on the lady's face, she turned to Dawn and said, "How can I help you?"

"My name is Dawn Star and I'm here to visit inmate Dakota Deer," Dawn said.

"Inmate Deer, hang on just a second." As the lady typed in the information Dawn noticed her name on her badge, Sargent H. Morningstar.

"Yes, here you are. You have a weekend visit with inmate Deer. Let me have him paged and someone will bring him up to the office."

"Thank you," Dawn said.

"If you'd like to have a seat, it will be just a few minutes," Sargent Morningstar said.

Taking one of the chairs over in the waiting area, Dawn noticed how busy everyone in the office was. She had never seen so many state police at one time. With so many people all in the same large room, Dawn was surprised at how quiet it was with the exception of the phones ringing.

"Quite the sight, aren't they?" Dawn was startled at the voice, not realizing how engrossed she had become with it all. Looking up she saw the smile on Dakota's face. As he reached down and took her hand, he continued. "Why Miss Dawn, I do believe this is the first time you've been speechless."

"Dakota!" She was up on her feet and in his arms. "Oh Dakota." As he held her he whispered into her ear. "Honey, I've really missed you."

As Dakota broke the embrace, the whole room started to applause. "Thank you, thank you, now if you smart-butts don't mind, my wife and I will be leaving."

"Dakota?" Dawn said.

"Honey, I'm friends with most of these cops and they know how much I've looked forward to your visit. It's just their way of welcoming you and teasing me a bit. Let's go over to my apartment, I'd better check on our dinner before it burns."

"You made dinner?" Dawn teased.

"Yes Ma'am, I had to, I fired my cook last week," he said as he winked at her.

They left the office and stopped by Dawn's van. Dakota took Dawn's suitcase out and carried it over to his apartment for her. Once at the apartment front door, Dakota set the suitcase down and turned to Dawn. Surprising Dawn, he quickly swept her up off her feet and into his arms. "I love you,

Mrs. Deer," and then he gently kissed her.

"I love you, Dakota and always will," Dawn answered when the kiss ended.

He carried her into the apartment and held her in his arms while she took in the view. There were long stem roses in vases sitting around the living room. The aroma of the candles burning in sconces on the wall gave off a heavenly sent.

Dawn noticed pictures of Dakota with her and the children, from the last visit hanging on the wall. There were other pictures as well that Dawn had sent him of her and the children. As she looked around the living room she then noticed the cypress knee on the coffee table. Waiting for the moment for her to see it, Dakota walked over to the couch and sat down, keeping Dawn on his lap. He waited for her to read it and then he read it out loud to her.

"Love is long-suffering and kind, It bears all things, believes all things, Hopes all things, endures all things, Love never fails." As Dakota read this, tears started to well up in Dawn's eyes. He continued speaking, "The long stem rose is to remind you of the undying love I have for you, for no matter where you are or what you do, my love will be with you and always has. I have loved you, Dawn, since you were sixteen. How I wish I would have told you back then."

Hearing this, Dawn could no longer control the floodgates of her tears. With the freedom of being released, they traveled down in streams on her cheeks. Dawn started to say something but Dakota gently laid his finger on her lips.

"The white dove is to remind you of the faith and the hope, that someday this will all be over and behind us. We will be together Dawn, somehow, someway just never give up."

Dakota sat back on the couch, gathered Dawn in his arms and as she lay her head on his shoulder, he stroked her hair, kissed her fore- head and said, "I love you, Dawn." She reached up and touched his cheek; he bent his head down and gave her a gentle kiss. Dawn responded and to Dakota's surprise, she deepened the kiss.

When the kiss ended, Dawn looked deeply into Dakota's eyes and said, "Darling, take me down the road that two people in love travel."

Knowing of Dawn's abusive past and never wanting to hurt or scare her Dakota said, "Dawn, are you sure?"

Leaning up and giving him a deep kiss, she then said, "I always thought I knew what love was, but I've learned with you that I've never been in love before. I was in love with love. I now know the difference. Yes, Darling, I'm sure."

Without saying a word and Dawn still in his arms, Dakota stood up and carried Dawn into the bedroom. He gently laid her on the bed and kissed her. Dakota then sat on the edge of the bed, reached over to his nightstand and lit a candle. "Many times I've written letters to you from right here and from the light of this candle. I've often wondered what it would be like to see you in candle light." Sitting up, Dawn touched Dakota's arm.

"I remember in one of your letter's you told me that candle light was very romantic, but I had no idea how true that was until today."

Without another word, Dakota gently stroked Dawn's cheek, leaned towards her and lightly kissed her lips. As the kissed deepened, they found themselves embraced in each other's arms and laying on the bed.

A few hours later when Dakota woke up, he found Dawn peacefully a sleep. Wondering if there would be anything left to the dinner he had made, Dakota slipped out of bed and put his pants on. Walking towards the bedroom door, Dakota turned back to look at Dawn. In the soft glow of the candlelight, Dakota thought she looked like an angel.

Once in the kitchen, Dakota checked on their dinner. Seeing the pot roast was still in good shape, Dakota started to peel potatoes. Deep in his own thoughts, Dakota never heard Dawn as she approached the kitchen door. Leaning on the door casing with Dakota's back towards her, Dawn stood as quite as a mouse for a moment. Not being able to resist any longer Dawn said, "I have always thought a man half dressed and cooking in the kitchen was a sexy site."

The sound of Dawn's voice stopped Dakota from peeling the potatoes. He turned around to face her. She was dressed in one of his flannel shirts, which hung down a few inches above her knees. She had rolled the sleeves up above her elbows. Taking in the sight of Dawn, Dakota smiled. "Darling that shirt never looked that good on me."

"I was hoping you wouldn't mind that I borrowed it, because I seemed to have misplaced my clothes," Dawn said with a smile. Turning red, Dakota remembered Dawn's suitcase was still out by the front door. As Dakota walked towards Dawn he said, "I think I know where they might be, but I kinda like what you have on now." Acting like a model, Dawn turned and said, "This year's sleep-wear is made of the finest flannel. One size fits all and it will be sure to drive your man crazy. The price is on this item is the cost of going to the closet."

Taking Dawn in his arms, he quickly kissed her and released her and then went to the front door. Picking up the suitcase and setting it in the living room, Dakota said, "I guess you won't be needing this for the weekend." Seeing the serious look on Dawn's face, Dakota walked over to Dawn. "Honey, I'm just teasing you about your clothes. I don't plan on having you run around all weekend in just a flannel." When Dawn didn't answer him, Dakota noticed she was looking at his chest, right above his heart. Realizing, he had never told her about his tattoo, and the bedroom had been to dark for her to have seen it. He knew she must be shocked, "Dawn, are you all right?"

Looking up and into Dakota's eyes Dawn softly asked, "Dakota, how long have you had this tattoo?"

"Darling, I put this tattoo on years ago when I was in the Air Force. I've known for many years that there was only one woman I would ever love." Saying the words to her inscribed on his chest, "I will love you forever, Dawn." Dakota gently kissed her. "Now Mrs. Deer, I think I'd better finish our dinner before I over cook the roast."

Stunned that Dakota had loved her for so many years and not knowing really what to say she replied, "Yes, Mr. Deer. I am kinda hungry." Dawn smiled at him. "I wouldn't want to keep the chef from doing his work."

In the kitchen, Dakota pulled out a chair at the table for Dawn to sit down. He then lit the candle in the centerpiece. While Dakota went and put the finishing touches on their dinner, Dawn had admired the table setting. The wine glasses even had, "Dakota & Dawn," etched on them. "Dakota, how did you get these wine glasses?"

He walked back to the table with their plates, and sitting them down, he then opened the bottle of wine that had been chilling on ice. "We have an inmate that etches on glass. He does beautiful pictures on mirrors, windows, just about anything that's glass. I asked him to make these for us."

Dakota poured the red wine into the glasses. "They're beautiful. It must have taken him quit a while to do them. The wine in them really brings out all the detail," Dawn said in awe.

Dakota sat down next to Dawn, "Honey, there's one more thing I need to show you." Reaching into his pocket, he pulled out a small gray ring box. As he opened the box and turned it towards Dawn he continued, "A while ago I asked you what your ring size was, I had told you that I wanted to make you a wedding ring. I sent to Europe for the finest silver and with all my love I've made this for you." Taking the ring out of the box and slipping it on Dawn's finger, he said, "Darling, you've been my wife for some time now, and I'd like the world to know you're a married woman."

"Oh Dakota, the ring is beautiful and I know you keep telling me that I'm you wife, but Darling, I really want to be your wife," Dawn said as her eyes filled with tears. Seeing that Dawn didn't understand

Dakota went on, "Dawn, we are married. We have been for over a year now. I thought you knew that."

"In my heart Dakota, I feel like I'm your wife, but I want to have your name and really be Mrs. Dakota Deer," Dawn said.

"Oh Sweetheart, you are and you do. I guess I never explained it to you. Here in the South, we have a law; it's called Common Law marriage. It's just as real as if we went before a preacher."

"Dakota, how can that be? I've heard of common law marriage, but I always thought two people had to live together for a certain amount of time. And Dakota, we've never lived together."

"Each state's requirements for common law marriage are different. This state requires only a few things. When you and I had met these requirements, I applied for our common law marriage license." Seeing the surprise on Dawn's face, Dakota gave her a quick kiss. "Wait right here, I'll go get it and show you." As Dakota left the kitchen, Dawn's hands started to shake. She picked up her wine glass and took a drink, hoping it would calm her down. She then decided a cigarette might help. When Dakota returned with the marriage license, he sat down at the table. "Darling, look at this. I think you'll be pleased." He handed her the envelope with the words Marriage License on the front of it.

As Dawn opened the envelope and pulled out the paper, her hands were still shaking. When she unfolded the paper and saw it was a marriage license, her mouth dropped open. Looking it over, seeing the magistrate's signature and the state seal, the tears in Dawn's eyes started down her cheeks. "Dakota, we're really married."

Taking the marriage license out of her hands and laying it on the table, Dakota took Dawn's hand in his. "Honey, I hope you'll forgive me for not sending this to you. It's just that I wanted to show it to you in person. This is your copy of our marriage license." Leaning towards Dawn, Dakota gently kissed her. "I love you Mrs. Dakota Deer. Please tell me that you're happy."

"At this moment Dakota, nothing could make me happier. To know I'm you're wife means everything to me."

"I think a toast to the bride and groom is in order," Dakota said as he handed Dawn her wine glass. Then taking his wine glass and putting it next to hers, he continued. "Love is long-suffering and kind. It bears all things, believes all things, hopes all things, and endures all things. Love never fails." Clicking their wine glasses together, they took a drink to their toast.

"Now Mrs. Deer. I don't know about you, but I am starving. What do you think, shall we eat?"

"Hmm, it smells and looks so good, it would be really sad to leave it," Dawn said with a smile.

In Washington, D.C. the President was looking over papers on his desk, when a knock at the door interrupted his thoughts. "Come in."

The door opened to the oval office and his secretary entered. "Mr. President as you requested, I have the governor of Louisiana on line one for you."

"Thank you, Sarah. Would you please see to it that I'm not disturbed for the rest of the day?"

"Yes Sir." As Sarah was closing the door to the oval office she said, "Have a good evening, Sir."

Taking a deep breath, the President picked up the phone. "Governor, thank you for holding."

"Yes, Sir, what can I do for you Mr. President?"

"You have an agent of mine living at the state police barracks. Dakota Deer. I want the man re-assigned."

"Sir, Agent Deer is to be leaving on an overseas assignment in three months. He's to be gone for a year."

"No, I've changed my mind. He's being reassigned. This is what I want you to do..." As the President explained what he wanted the governor listened, he finished by saying, "...and I want this all done tonight."

"Yes Sir, Mr. President, but Agent Deer is spending the weekend with his wife. He won't be happy that we'll be interrupting him."

"Governor, Agent Deer is very dedicated to his country. When duty calls, everything else must wait," the President said.

"I'll get right on it Sir. Have a good evening."

"Good evening to you, Governor."

A few hours later as midnight approached....

"I love you Dawn," Dakota said as he kissed her neck and rolled over to his side of the bed, he put his arm out. "Come over here and let me hold you."

Dawn moved over into Dakota's arms. As she laid her head on his chest, she wrapped her arm around him. "I love you, Dakota. I think we should stay right here the rest of the weekend."

"Hmm, sounds good to me," Dakota said softly.

Just then someone started knocking on Dakota's front door. When Dakota didn't move and the person at the door persisted with the knocking, Dakota said to Dawn, "Stay right here, Honey, I'll be right back." As he pulled on his jeans he looked back at Dawn, "This had better be good. Everyone knows not to disturb me this weekend." Without saying a word Dawn watched as Dakota left the room.

As Dakota opened the door, he saw Chew standing there. "Chew what the hell ya doing here? You know I don't want to be bothered!"

"I know, but it's an emergency. Captain Miller needs to see you in his office," Chew said.

Taking a deep breath and letting it out Dakota said, "All right Chew. Tell him I'll be there in ten minutes." Chew nodded and walked away.

Closing the door, Dakota walked back to the bedroom. "Dakota, is everything all right?" Dawn said sounding worried.

With his back turned towards Dawn, Dakota pulled a clean shirt out of the closet. "Honey, everything's fine. The captain needs to see me. I'll be gone for just a little while." Pulling his shirt on, he sat on the bed and reached for his boots. "You'll be safe here. It's been a long day for you, why don't you try and get a little sleep." Turning towards Dawn he took her in his arms, gave her a kiss and said. " I'll be back as soon as I can."

"I'll miss you Dakota," Dawn said with a small yawn. Getting up and walking towards the door, Dakota looked back. "I love you, Angel." But before Dawn could answer he was gone.

Dawn snuggled down into the blankets and thought to herself, *"Maybe I'll just rest my eyes for a little."* And then she fell a sleep.

Entering the captain's office, Dakota noticed Chew, the captain and the governor leaning over a map. As he approached closer, he could see it was a map of Michigan. "No, it's not Crystal Mountain. It's called Crystal Valley," Chew said to the men. "Are you sure? Chew I don't see a Crystal Valley on the map," the governor said.

"That's because it's too small to be on the map. Hell, Dakota once told me they don't even have their own post office. Guess it's a ghost town," Chew said.

"Gentlemen, I really hate to interrupt this map reading lesson. But would someone please tell me what the hell is going on?" Dakota said with anger in his voice.

"We're talking about where you grew up," Captain Miller replied. Hearing this for an answer Dakota went from a little angry to boiling. "Let me get this straight. You three got me out of bed with my wife, to find out where I grew up? Do you all have a fuckin death wish? Because if you do, I believe it could be arranged!"

Seeing the anger on Dakota's face Captain Miller said, "Governor, now would be a good time to show Dakota the paper." Handing Dakota the paper the governor said, "Dakota you're being reassigned. You leave tomorrow."

Dakota yelled, "Tomorrow? I'm not going anywhere tomorrow! In case ya'll forgot my wife is here for the weekend. I've given up many things for my country, but I'm not giving up this weekend! I don't care if the President ordered my new assignment, it will wait until my wife leaves!"

"Dakota, just look at the paper in your hand," Chew said. Reading the paper over, Dakota looked up at the governor. "Governor, what is this? What the hell do I need a pardon for? We all know I'm not really an inmate. I don't need this to go on my assignments." With that said, Dakota tossed the pardon on the table with the map.

"You do for this one," the governor said smiling, "Dakota you're going home with your wife." Speechless at hearing this, Dakota sat down. "Your next assignment is in Michigan. Your cover will be a married man with four children. Since you have that part already taken cared of, that shouldn't be a problem for you. There is no danger in this assignment for your family, but as always there will be agents keeping surveillance on them. You're to take the next six months, get settled, find a local job and then contact Washington. By the way, the President did order this assignment for you. Now do you still have a problem taking this assignment by tomorrow?"

Taking in what the governor had said, Dakota didn't know what to say. "Well would ya look at that? I do believe this is the first time I've seen Agent Deer not sure what to do with an assignment," Chew said laughing.

"Fuck you, Chew," Dakota said, then looking at the governor he continued, "Governor, how long did the President say this assignment was for?"

"I asked the President the same thing. I knew you wouldn't like it if it were only for a few months. Don't worry Dakota, the President is aware how something like this could mess with an agent's mind. The assignment is permanent. You will have a lot more freedom to work for your country this way," the governor said. "Now if you gentlemen don't mind, it's late and I'm sure Dakota would like to get back to his wife."

Standing up and shaking the governor's hand Dakota said, "It's been a pleasure, Sir." Captain Miller walked over to Dakota shook his hand, smiled and said, "Inmate Deer, get the hell out of my office."

As Dakota walked towards the door he looked at Chew and said, "Chew, I'll talk to you later."

"Dakota, you forgetting something?" Chew said as he picked up the pardon off the table and waved it. "I think you might want to show this to your wife tonight."

Dakota walked back to Chew and taking the paper from him, he said, "Thanks bro, I'm sure glad to have you for a partner."

Chew handed Dakota the paper and said, "Get out of here, Agent Deer. I believe you next assignment is waiting for you."

Standing in the doorway of the bedroom, Dakota noticed the candle was still burning, causing a soft glow on Dawn. Smiling at the angel he saw before him, Dakota walked towards the bed. As he gently sat down on the bed, Dawn stirred in her sleep, "Dakota," she said.

"I'm here Angel," Dakota whispered in her ear and then kissed her cheek. Her eyes slowly fluttered open. Seeing Dakota she smiled, "Is everything all right?"

"Everything's fine Darling." Dakota paused, "Are you awake? I want to show you something."

"Yes, I'm awake. What is it Dakota?" Dawn said with a small yawn. Dakota reached over to the lamp on the nightstand. "Watch your eye's, I'm going to turn on the lamp."

"Ok, I'm ready." Dawn said. Dakota turned on the lamp and as Dawn's eyes adjusted to the light, Dakota held the paper so Dawn could read it. When Dawn was done reading it, she sat up in bed, her heart was pounding, "Dakota, does this mean what I think it means?" Silently, to herself she said, *"Dear God, please let him say yes."*

Dakota smiled and gently kissed her, "Well Mrs. Deer, according to the great state of Louisiana, I'm now a free man, but I will always be a prisoner of the heart."

Printed in the United States
1434600001B/284